Crabs in a Barrel

Also by Byron Harmon

Mistakes Men Make
All The Women I've Loved

Crabs in a Barrel

Byron Harmon

To Shirley
I hope you find this Book
funny

AGATE

Chicago

Printed in Canada.

Library of Congress Cataloging-in-Publication Data

Harmon, Byron.
    Crabs in a barrel / by Byron Harmon.
        p. cm.
    Summary: "Comic adventure of a yacht-full of African Americans ship-
    wrecked on their way to the Bahamas, who must learn to survive without
    killing each other."—Provided by publisher.
        ISBN-13: 978-1-932841-21-3 (pbk.)
        ISBN-10: 1-932841-21-0 (pbk.)
        1. African Americans—Fiction. 2. Shipwrecks—Fiction. I. Title.
        PS3608.A748C73 2006
        813'.6—dc22
        2005036684

This novel is a work of fiction. Names, characters, incidents, and dialogue, except
for incidental references to public figures, products, or services, are imaginary
and are not intended to refer to any living persons or to disparage any company's
products or services.

To my parents,
David and Shirley Harmon

Acknowledgments

There have been so many people who have been a part of my literary journey. It was a long, slow, and sometimes frustrating trip. You were by my side as I sold *All the Women I've Loved,* my first self-published novel, out of the trunk of my car. You helped me plan the parties where hundreds of people danced the night away, like at the release party for *Mistakes Men Make.* You shared my joy when I got my first book deal with a major publishing house. I could never properly thank you for all of your support. Just know that my success is your success.

I want to thank my brothers, Andre and Marshall. I want to thank my beautiful girlfriend, Rhadia Hursey. I want to thank my brothers from another mother: Doug Bennett, Eric Delvillar, Mike Wilson, Gregory Blue, Marcus Virgil, Drak Muse, Big Ryal, Shannon Lanier, and Craig Johnson. My own review team, sisters Kay and Kelly. I want to thank The Roots Book Club and Carey Yazeed and Mary Mitchell. My longtime friends Jennifer Wiggins, Shon Gables, Lauren Petterson, and Corrin Johnson. I want to thank Selena James for teaching me how to edit. I want to thank Angie Henderson at Adeeva Publicity. Also, the lovely ladies of Pentouch.com. Thanks to Kim Hines and Tia Shabazz. You were there from the start.

I want to thank Doug Seibold and Agate for believing in this project. And I want to thank my agent, Lane Zachary, for believing in me.

Chapter One

SAHARA HAWTHORNE HATED shaking her ass for money. While she wasn't really *shaking her ass* in the traditional sense, bartending fancy yacht parties felt about one step *up* from sliding *down* the pole. She knew that posh caterers paid top-dollar as much for her looks as for her serving skills. Now that she was twenty-seven, Sahara had already spent the past few years trying to downplay her career as a former college beauty queen. But rich customers always spent more when the help was attractive, and she didn't care because she had some major student loan bills to pay. *Really* major.

Sahara looked at her watch and sighed. *Two more hours to go. I can't wait until we get to the Bahamas.*

As she smoothed the formfitting black miniskirt over her hips, Sahara flashed her most authentic phony smile. *But if just one more of these bougie-ass Negroes winks at me or tries to brush up against my butt, I'ma push somebody overboard.*

The luxury charter yacht, *The King's Dream*, had been out to sea for only an hour but Sahara's high-heeled size-sevens already hurt. The hard-partying passengers kept her and Shannon, the other cater-waitress, hopping. The yacht was part of a small fleet headed to a weekend birthday and gambling party at the Atlantis Resort in the Bahamas. It was rumored that the host, a major basketball star, spent more than a quarter of a million dollars renting out the charter yachts to taxi his guests. The partiers came from all over the country, an eclectic mix of celebrities, invited guests, a few radio contest winners, and—of course—groupies. *The King's Dream* was the last ship to leave Miami and was running an hour behind the rest of the yachts, thanks to Ethan Murphy, its late and very hungover captain.

"Ah choo!" Murphy's nose had been tingling all morning. He squinted and massaged his throbbing temples. Captain Murphy's head ached from a night of too much Captain Morgan with coke (*not* of the cola variety). He had a miserable expression on his face as Shannon handed him a bottle of water and two Tylenols.

"You look terrible, Captain Murphy," she cracked. "And your uniform has more wrinkles than a ninety-year-old white woman."

Captain Murphy ignored her comment and gulped the first pill. It felt like he was swallowing an entire dinner roll. "I have to stop this," he muttered.

He had better. The owner of the charter line had given the fifty-three-year old captain an ultimatum: *"Be on time or next time be out of a job."* Captain Murphy was lucky that there were few private boat captains who could navigate the tricky waters of the Caribbean as well as he did, or he would have been forced down the plank a long time ago. Standing on the bridge, he tried to soak up the cool salt air. The scene was breathtaking. The sun was burning away any chance of a cloudy sky. As far as the eye could see were miles upon miles of clear blue water punctuated here and there by sea gulls diving into the waves, snatching sea snacks from the depths. Captain Murphy took a deep breath and smiled at a school of dolphins that were racing alongside the yacht.

It's so peaceful out here I could die, the captain thought.

He marveled at the ease with which the yacht sliced through the water. Powered by twin 1500-horsepower engines, *The King's Dream* was a modern maritime masterpiece. It was eighty-four feet long and could sleep sixteen people comfortably. In the cabin below was the large galley, which boasted a huge stainless steel Viking oven and deep freezer. Further back was the lounge area, aptly nicknamed "The Lap of Luxury." It was decorated with expensively comfortable sofas and chairs, with matching coffee and end tables in deep mahogany. If all that furniture was removed—along with the 52-inch plasma flat-screen TV and home theater system—the entire group of passengers could dance the Electric Slide there with ease. Above deck was the "Sky Lounge," where passengers could relax in the open air.

Wolf Bailey, one of the passengers, lounged in front of the TV set. "Damn," he mumbled, rubbing his stomach like an expectant mother. "I can't wait until we get to the Bahamas."

The constant rocking and sloshing was making him seasick. Tall and slender, Wolf was attractive in a dark and menacing kind of way. He was the kind of man who reminded women that Satan was once an angel, too. The cold, smooth black of Wolf's skin matched his eyes. There was violence in them. Wolf came up on the gritty streets of Brooklyn, and he was a lot more at home on subways than yachts. He had thought a trip to the Bahamas would relax him. Besides, he *needed* to be out of town right now, considering what was about to go down back home. Wolf motioned for Fat Black, his bodyguard, to follow him up to the Sky Lounge for a smoke. Maybe a blunt in the open sea air would settle his stomach. As they left, Wolf winked at the pair of attractive women standing by the spiral staircase. Rachel and Valerie Mims smiled backed nervously. Once Wolf was out of earshot, Valerie playfully licked her lips. "Damn girl, he fine as Tupac."

Rachel gave her cousin a knowing nod. "Is he a rapper?"

Her cousin shrugged, then grinned. "I don't know, but I'd like to *wrap* my legs around his back."

Rachel stole a glance upstairs. "Girl, he must be somebody."

"Why?" Valerie frowned.

"Cuz, he got a bodyguard."

There were three things the Mims girls knew and cared about: men, money, and men with money. Unemployed at the moment, they were short on all three. However, since they were blessed with the bodies and looks of a pair of Luke dancers, Rachel and Valerie could always scrape up enough money from sugar daddies to make the scene. It didn't matter if it was the *Soul Train* or *Source* awards, you could almost always find the pair of them, decked out in tight dresses and holding on to the arms of other hangers-on.

"Here are your drinks, ladies," Sahara smiled.

"I ordered a Long Island Iced Tea—*this* looks like a margarita," Valerie snapped. "Can't you get a simple order right?"

Sahara gritted her teeth. "My mistake, miss." Then, in her best Victor Newman voice, she said, "I could have sworn that when you insisted that I line the rim of the glass with salt because that's how you liked your margaritas, it was because you wanted a margarita."

Valerie jerked her head toward Rachel. "No she didn't?"

"Girl, calm down," Rachel said. "Don't ruin our trip over a damn waitress."

Sahara ignored the comment and walked over to a short brother snickering in the corner. Clearly, he had overheard her exchange with the two cousins. He gave her a knowing wink. Sahara smiled. The guy looked like someone's little brother who was lost at the mall.

"Sir, would you like a drink?"

"Uh, yeah," he said, loud enough for Rachel and Valerie to hear. "I'd like a Long Island Iced Tea. And, uh, add a little margarita to it."

Rachel and Valerie rolled their eyes.

"Think you're a comedian, huh?" Sahara joked.

"That's what I'm getting paid for," he said.

Sahara looked confused.

"Oh, I'm performing tonight at the big party," he explained while extending his hand. "It's my big break. Name's Fame."

"I'm Sahara. Nice to meet you, uh, Fame."

He leaned over and whispered, "Sahara, huh? You look more like an oasis to me."

"Goodbye," Sahara snapped. She took off in the direction of a couple sitting on a couch who were waving her over.

"Can I get you two a mixed drink?" she asked.

"Oh no, my sister," the dark-skinned man replied, slightly offended. He adjusted his kufi. "We don't pollute our bodies with liquor." He looked at the woman next to him. "We'd like a couple of glasses of spring water."

Sahara gave him a look that no man should have to endure. But instead of snapping on him, she gathered her composure and said politely, "I'll be right back."

"Now Muhammad, why do you always have to be so rude?" the woman turned and asked.

"Shon, she just assumed that we drink liquor," he said.

She threw up her hands in protest. "Well, here we are on a party boat! I wonder why she'd think that?"

Muhammad frowned. "We're not even supposed to be here. Now we're only going to have one day alone and all to ourselves."

"Are you blaming me?" Shon snapped. "I'm not the one who *had* a friend who *had* a hookup on some plane tickets."

"Don't be sarcastic, Shon."

"Everything isn't a conspiracy," she said.

"Whatever," Muhammad said. "What about that Uncle Tom over there in the corner?"

"How do you know he's an Uncle Tom?" Shon frowned.

"Did you see how he was kissing that white woman at the pier before we left?"

"And?" Shon said.

"It's house niggers like him who fall victim to the biggest conspiracy of them all."

Shon sighed. "And what conspiracy is that?"

Mumammad sucked his teeth. "The conspiracy against the black man. Some brothers just don't feel that they are successful unless they have a white woman."

"Muhammad, you need Jesus," Shon smiled.

The "Uncle Tom" he was talking about was named Samuel, but his good friends at the Woodmore Country Club just outside of Washington DC—even his white friends—called him Sammy. From the moment Sammy stepped on the boat he could feel the eyes of the other passengers watching him. Judging him as he longingly kissed his woman goodbye. His blonde, blue-eyed beauty of a white woman. He got a kick out of the looks, especially the "death threat" glares from black women. *Whatever,* he thought. They'd had their chance. They hadn't wanted him when he was a struggling student working two menial jobs. He was too black, too skinny, too ugly. Now that he was a successful corporate lawyer with a beautiful blonde girlfriend, they all wanted him. Well, too late—now he wanted Lauren. And he wanted a drink.

"Excuse me, waitress?" he called to Sahara.

Sahara motioned for Shannon to help Sammy. She was too busy trying to get another order straight.

Confused, Sahara said, "Lemme get this right, sir."

"The name's Jean-Paul Baptiste," the handsome curly-headed brother said, flashing a thousand-watt smile.

"Uh…okay, Jean-Paul," she smiled back. "You want a double shot of Jose Cuervo on the rocks and a spritz of Coke?"

"And a spritz of lemon juice, and don't forget to stir it—three times," Jean-Paul added.

"Okaaay… I'll be right back with that, then," Sahara said, and then winced after she turned around. *He's going to need a Pepto-Bismol chaser after drinking that.*

"Hurry back," he said biting his lip. Watching her walk away, Jean-Paul briefly contemplated breaking off his engagement with his fiancé Nicollete. He looked down at the vibrating message on his cell phone.

Jesus. Nikki again? It was her fourth message today.

Nikki had been dead set against him taking this trip. The couple had argued for days, but it was nothing compared to the battle royal Jean-Paul had fought with his father, Henri, a prominent New Orleans judge who was constantly reminding Jean-Paul about his family obligations. But how could he turn down the bachelor party in the Bahamas that Mike Wilson, his best friend and former 82nd Airborne Army buddy, had planned for him? Mike lived in New York City and it had been nearly a year since they had seen each other. Jean-Paul was looking forward to the reunion—and to the strippers. After all, in less than two weeks Jean-Paul would be a married man.

I'll listen to Nikki then, he grinned.

Meanwhile, on the upper deck, Wolf blew a thick plume of smoke into the cool sea air. He and Fat Black were at the very back of the boat so the others wouldn't catch a whiff of their pungent chronic.

"This time tomorrow," Wolf coughed, offering the tightly rolled blunt to Fat Black, "I will have the best connect on the East Coast." Wolf's eyes were a demonic blood-red from the smoke. The burly bodyguard waved him off. "C'mon, Wolf, you know I don't smoke."

Wolf shrugged and took another huge toke. "Nigga, you should, because this right here," he held the blunt up to the sky, "is some bomb-ass weed."

"Hey boss, you think this dude Nigel you're meeting is on the up and up?"

Wolf laughed. "If he ain't, he gon' be six feet *under.*"

Forty-five minutes later, Captain Murphy gave a final check to his gauges and sat back in the captain's chair. *Everything looks good,* he thought as he stretched out. But everything wasn't good. Unbeknownst to Captain Murphy, fumes were slowly escaping from a ruptured propane line. The propane lines ran from the engine room through a series of ducts that led to the galley. The cool ocean air had carried the leaking scent out to sea. Down below in the galley, Fat Black was fetching his boss an ice-cold Corona from the refrigerator, where he paused to ask Shannon if they had anything to eat other than finger foods.

"What do you want, some Popeyes?" she quipped, then quickly caught herself. "Um, please give me a second, sir," she frowned while turning the gas on the oven. *Ugh, she thought. I can't wait until we get to the Baha—*

Before Shannon finished her sentence, the oven—along with an entire section of the galley—exploded. Shannon and Fat Black were killed instantly as the fireball blew out the portholes and flames began consuming everything in the immediate area. The yacht shook violently before lurching to one side, weighted down by the water that rushed instantly into the gaping hole. *The King's Dream* looked as if the greatest of great white sharks had taken a huge bite out of her. Belowdecks, passengers and furniture were tossed around like toys. Flames fueled by the thick new paint coating the interior walls raced along the sides of the room, charring the carpet and drapes. The passengers panicked, scrambling over each other in a desperate dash to escape. Up top, Captain Murphy was thrown backwards by the blast, his head bouncing against a railing and then caroming back off of the instrument console in front of him. Momentarily dazed, he needed a few seconds to comprehend what was happening. Wiping the blood from the nasty cut above his brow, he saw the huge hole and thick black smoke billowing from the side of the ship. Murphy immediately realized that all chance of continued sailing was lost. He had to make a quick decision. Should he radio a Mayday or unwinch the lifeboat? Years of experience had taught him that in a situation like this, he only had minutes, maybe seconds, before the entire ship sank. Murphy ran to the lifeboat and feverishly started uncranking the winch. Wolf, who had nearly been thrown overboard and was just now getting his bearings, saw what the captain was doing and raced to assist him. It took less than thirty seconds for the lifeboat to splash down to the ocean and Wolf was the first one to jump in. Murphy turned to run back toward the radio. He was instantly flattened by one of the passengers racing toward him. It was Sammy. He looked at Murphy with panic in his eyes.

"The lifeboat's over there," Murphy motioned him toward the ladder. Meanwhile, screams and coughing were coming from below. After standing and dusting himself off, Murphy reached his hand into the smoky staircase to pull out first Valerie and then Rachel, who clung to her cousin for dear life. Once on deck they cried while sucking in deep gulps of air. Fame was the next to come up, coughing, his face blackened from the smoke. He looked like a minstrel comic.

"Anybody else alive down there?" Murphy asked him.

"D-don't know," Fame stuttered as he gasped for air.

Murphy carefully stepped down the stairs, waving smoke away from his face. He bumped into Muhammad and Shon slowly coming up. They were gripping the railings. Murphy helped them to the deck and then pulled up a very woozy Jean-Paul.

"Get in the lifeboat," Murphy yelled to the confused passengers standing on the deck. "She's gonna sink soon." He knew that the main reason there was so much smoke was because the seawater was dousing the flames. That was both good and bad. The hundreds of gallons of water *The King's Dream* was taking on helped kill the fire but also caused the ship to list dangerously. Murphy cracked his knuckles. As the passengers clambered into the lifeboat, Jean-Paul scanned the chaos for Sahara.

Where is she? he thought. He turned and ran back toward the stairs.

"Did you find the waitresses?" he asked Murphy, who grabbed for him.

"No," he said, pulling Jean-Paul's arm. "It's too late. We have to get on the lifeboat. C'mon, we're about to sink."

Jean-Paul pushed him away and ran down below deck. The smoke almost overwhelmed him. He dropped to the floor, pulling off his shirt and holding it to his mouth to help him breathe. Jean-Paul had a decent line of vision at that level and he quickly scanned for Sahara. The right side of the boat was rising slowly as it took on more and more water. He had to act fast or he would be trapped in the boat as it sank. Then Jean-Paul caught sight of Sahara's feet sticking out from behind the bar. The bar had crashed backwards against the mirrored wall, trapping her under its splintered frame. As Jean-Paul crawled towards her he could hear Sahara's muffled groans.

"Are you okay?" he yelled.

"Please help me," she moaned.

Jean-Paul lifted the bar and Sahara managed to climb out, her hands bleeding from tiny nicks and cuts. After letting the bar crash back down, Jean-Paul led her to the stairs. Her legs hurt, but Sahara was able to jump onto his back and he hauled them both above decks. They cautiously made their way to the boat's edge, where Jean-Paul helped Sahara down the ladder to the waiting passengers.

Sahara's eyes darted around the boat. Shannon was missing. "Where's Shannon? She was the other server on board," she asked. "Where is she?"

The passengers were silent and avoided her gaze.

"No, no," Sahara cried.

Her cries quickly turned into a scream because, as Jean-Paul was climbing down, the right side of the *The King's Dream* shot straight upright, throwing him headfirst nearly ten feet over the lifeboat into the water.

"Oh, no," someone yelled, as the passengers scurried to the boat's edge.

Jean-Paul furiously splashed water with his arms. "Help, I can't—" he gurgled. A wave overtook him and he disappeared. Seconds later, Jean-Paul's head and splashing arms popped up just a few yards away.

"There," Sahara pointed. "He's over there."

Murphy reached out with an oar and pulled Jean-Paul into the lifeboat. Once Jean-Paul was safely inside, a tremendous wave rocked their tiny lifeboat. It was the wake thrown off by *The King's Dream* sinking beneath the surface. All the passengers could see was the horizon and a few scattered suitcases floating around them in the water like apples bobbing in a barrel. They managed to scoop up a few of the smaller bags. For a long time everyone was silent as the magnitude of their situation dawned on them. They were alone and lost at sea.

Chapter Two

ABOUT THE ONLY WONDER PARADISE ISLAND doesn't have is Wonder Woman. The travel brochures should have renamed the Bahamian resort Fantasy Island, because it looked like the kind of place where everyone's dreams could come true. Located in Nassau, The Bahamas, Paradise Island, along with the megaresort Atlantis, has long been a playground for the rich, the famous, and the pleasure seeking. It has everything a vacationer could want: crystal-clear beaches, world-class golf courses, and casinos that rival those of Las Vegas. In fact, Atlantis is sometimes called the "Vegas of the Caribbean" and gambling is what most of the guests for the NBA star's big party came to do. As the fleet of yachts began to arrive in Nassau Harbor, the passengers stampeded toward the casinos, a herd of giddy gamblers fatted for the slaughter.

Meanwhile, there was still no sign of *The King's Dream* or her passengers.

Murphy should have been here by now, thought Johnnie Doyle, the crotchety fleet captain. He was getting nervous, especially with a nasty storm brewing to the south. Doyle was an old-school mariner who walked with a limp and looked more like a pirate than a respectable captain. Doyle deep down felt himself to be a throwback to the great early ocean explorers, like Magellan and Columbus. There was nothing he liked more than to chart a course by the stars, and he felt equally at home in a fifteen-foot catboat, a diesel-powered pleasure yacht, or an eighty-foot high-tech racing sailboat. He sat on the bridge of his own yacht, *The Good Ship Jesus,* attempting to chart Murphy's position on the map. Doyle had radioed him more than a dozen times to no avail. The last transmission from Captain Murphy had come when he was about an hour outside Miami. Doyle hated Murphy's work ethic but loved that he had a bit of that old-time salty swagger in him. It wasn't uncommon for Murphy to be late, but this was troubling. Doyle took off his cap and scratched his bald head. He focused on the dark storm clouds gathering on the horizon, then grabbed his radio.

"Coast Guard One, this is *The Good Ship Jesus*...Over," Doyle barked.

A few seconds later, a voice crackled through the static.

"*Good Ship Jesus,* this is Coast Guard One copy, over."

"I have a ship in my group, *The King's Dream,* which is MIA, over."

"Copy, *The King's Dream* MIA. What was her SP and ST? Over."

"Starting point was Miami and starting time was 14:30, over," Doyle said reaching for the charts and sail plan.

"I copy SP Miami and ST 14:30, how many is she carrying? Over."

"She had twelve on board, over."

"I copy twelve on board. I'm scrambling a bird. I'll need you to fax the sail plan, over."

"Copy," Doyle answered. He listened to the thunder rolling in the distance and hoped he was overreacting.

Chapter Three

"I AM FUCKED," Muhammad muttered to himself. "I am so fucked."

"We're all fucked," Fame shot back at him.

Muhammad shared a knowing glance with Shon and slammed his fist down on the edge of the boat. "Trust me when I tell you that I am *royally* fucked."

As the tiny lifeboat rocked back and forth on the waves, the small crew of survivors looked more like shell-shocked combat soldiers than sailors. There was no shade from the sun and the temperature was at least 95 degrees, and the heat combined with the heavy humidity had them all sweating like runaway slaves. Murphy, the only one skilled at handling a boat in the open sea, was fading in and out of consciousness, as it became apparent that his head wounds had resulted in a concussion. The others were nursing various cuts and bruises. Surprisingly, the lifeboat's first-aid kit was well stocked and Sahara, trying to keep her mind off Shannon's death and the thought of their dangerous situation, took charge of treating their injuries with the skill of an emergency room doctor. Most of the passengers stared at her with blank expressions, still not believing their misfortune. A few silently prayed, some cried softly, the rest hoped. The thunder and lightning crackling in the distance added to their sense of desperation.

"Hey! This whole scene is like a black *Gilligan's Island*," Fame cracked, trying to relieve the tension.

His joke was greeted with silence.

"Damn, I feel like Elian Gonzalez," he continued, wiping sweat from his brow. "Where's Janet Reno when a nigga need her?"

"Shut the fuck up!" Wolf snapped. "Ain't shit funny about being stranded in the middle of nowhere."

Fame smacked his lips. "Who made you captain?"

"I made my damn self captain, what you gon' do about it?" Wolf glared.

Fame rolled his eyes. "Whatever."

"Y'all both need to chill out," Jean-Paul chimed in. "This situation is jacked up enough. We need to stick together and figure how we gon' survive."

"Oh yeah?" Wolf turned to Jean-Paul. "You got a survival plan? Who you supposed to be, MacGyver?"

Before Jean-Paul had a chance to respond, Sammy jumped in. "My brothers, my brothers, calm down, please." Sammy's nervous voice was high and squeaky. "We need to stay united. If we gon' make it, we need to get along."

The other men laughed, and even Wolf snickered.

"What's so funny?" Sammy asked.

"We need to get along?" Fame mocked. "Thank you, Rodney King!" This time the entire crew laughed, even the ones who were crying. The laughter seemed to quell the tension for the time being. But Jean-Paul and Wolf continued to stare coldly at each other.

Valerie winced at the nasty cut on her arm. The blood had dried and caked on the squiggly scar that ran along her caramel-colored forearm. She was about to reach over and wash it in the warm ocean water.

"You shouldn't do that," Sahara warned.

Valerie ignored her and began sticking her fingers in the water.

"I'm telling you," Sahara warned again.

"You're telling me what?" Valerie snapped. "I know how to clean a damn cut. You are supposed to wash it." She shook her head in disgust. "Anyway, what do you know? And why are you playing nursemaid? You're a damn waitress."

The group looked at Sahara. They were like fans at a tennis match and if they were keeping score in the match between these two women, the score would be *no love.*

"Look here, bitch," Sahara said standing to throw a bloody bandage in the water. Jean-Paul was impressed that she managed to stand straight up on the wobbly lifeboat. Sahara cut a striking figure. She had their full attention.

"For your information, I am not a waitress. I am a third-year surgical resident at Emory University Medical Center. Cater-waiting, *not* waitressing, is how I am paying off my enormous student loans." Sahara was pissed; a thick throbbing vein in her neck was clearly visible. "So go ahead and wash your cut in salty seawater, and when the *Vibrio vulnificus* bacteria infects your bloodstream and causes you excruciating stomach pains, septic shock, skin lesions, and liver failure, don't look at me. I'll just push your dead ass over the side of the lifeboat and let the sharks eat you."

Valerie snatched her arm out of the water.

"She's a doctor?" Rachel blurted out, while everyone else thought it.

"A resident—with more than a hundred hours in the OR."

"Shit," Fame mumbled. "You can open me up anytime."

The sight of a large gray form gliding nearby beneath the water's surface interrupted them.

"Look at the dolphin," Shon said, pointing at the large fin moving toward them fewer than twenty feet away. The passengers followed the fin wide-eyed as it began circling the tiny lifeboat.

"That's not a dolphin," Captain Murphy said groggily.

"Huh?" the crew said in unison. One by one they turned to stare at the captain. Fame gulped loudly.

"W-w-what is it?" Rachel asked nervously.

"That's a shark," the captain said, trying to reach for an oar.

Chapter Four

LIEUTENANT DON SHIRLEY PREPARED TO LIFT OFF for his second search-and-rescue mission of the day. On the first, it turned out that the so-called "stranded crew" had simply run out of gas, but judging by the slurring-voiced captain they encountered, they had plenty of liquor. As the helicopter took to the air, Lt. Shirley, a ten-year Coast Guard veteran, sighed and smiled—it was all in a day's work for the brave men and women of the 7th District.

When it comes to duty stations, it's hard to beat the Coast Guard. The United States Coast Guard's 7th District Headquarters is located in Miami but has a much larger area of responsibility. It also keeps track of the waters off South Carolina, Georgia, Florida, and the Caribbean. While the Coast Guard does routine law enforcement work like border patrols and drug interdiction, it's from search and rescue that it has earned the reputation of 'sea saviors.'

Shirley nodded as his co-pilot punched in the last known coordinates of *The King's Dream*. They hoped to spot the vessel or fly into range of its distress beacon. Lt. Shirley believed firmly he had one of the best and most experienced crews in the Coast Guard. On board were Bill Waxman, his copilot; T.J., the flight mechanic; and Ed Watts, called "Aquaman"—a crazy rescue diver who was experienced in many different environments, including high seas, surf, swift water, and even cliffs. The crew had been together for four years, during which time they had rescued more than two hundred people. Their helicopter, a Sikorsky Jayhawk, was a state-of-the-art medium-range recovery vehicle outfitted with all-weather electronics, infrared direction finders, night vision—the works.

It took the crew less than thirty minutes to lock on to the last known coordinates of *The King's Dream*. They planned to follow the charted course in a wide, sweeping, zigzag formation in order to maximize their field of vision. The weather was still clear in the immediate area and as the chopper sped over miles of the Atlantic, all the crew could see were miles of the Atlantic. Before long, they'd covered hundreds of square miles with no luck. The crew all began to fear that the ship must be lost. But how? Lt. Shirley wondered. It would take a catastrophe to sink that kind of yacht, given the way they were built these days. And why hadn't the captain sent out a Mayday radio call? A telltale beeping and blinking on the control panel interrupted the pilot's thoughts. It was the GPS, the chopper's satellite global positioning system, which they also used to pick up a ship's distress homing beacon. The beacon was suddenly pulsing very powerfully in the immediate area they were flying over. As they hovered, they scanned in every direction. Lt. Shirley double-checked the GPS's readings—they were dead on target. That's when Bill noticed the large circular oil slick. This could only mean one thing: the ship had sunk. The crew looked for floating debris or worse, bodies, but they all knew that if a boat her size had sunk hours ago, and in these swift currents, there would probably not be any sign left. The crew looked at each other but said nothing. The mission would now become a search and recovery effort, but it would have to be postponed for at least day.

The storm that was coming up was a big one.

Chapter Five

"**E**VERYBODY MOVE as close as they can to the center of the boat," Murphy commanded. "But do it slowly." It may have been a tiny lifeboat, but he was still its captain as long as he was conscious.

Everyone shuffled into position, though the bulky life vests complicated their movements. Their lives depended on it. They were scared witless.

"It must have been attracted by the bloody bandages," Sammy offered. "I saw a story on *Nationa—*"

"Shut up," Captain Murphy ordered through clenched teeth. "It's a tiger shark. Stay still and be very quiet."

Sammy cut his eyes at the captain.

The Atlantic waters off North America contain one of the world's biggest reserves of sharks. One of the prime inhabitants is the aggressive tiger shark. Growing to a weight of up to fourteen hundred pounds, this super-predator gets its name from the dark black spots and vertical bars that run along the length of its body. These spots glistened and were clearly visible as the large shark slowly circled, as if inspecting the boat. As soon as it appeared, the shark disappeared. The nervous survivors continued to huddle.

Maybe it went away?

After nearly thirty anxious seconds of holding their breath, they all sighed. They hoped the worst was over. It wasn't.

Thump! The boat rocked slightly. The sound came from beneath them. They sat frozen, with terror in their eyes. Everyone was silently praying, except for Murphy. He gripped his oar tighter.

A few seconds later, thump! The boat rocked again.

"What's it doing?" Sahara asked.

"Trying to figure out what this big solitary white object is," Captain Murphy explained. "It may think we're a dead whale."

It really didn't matter, because a tiger shark could eat damn near anything, including humans. After catching them in their nets, some fishermen claimed to have seen garbage cans inside their enormous stomachs. Murphy had no intentions of being fish food.

"Somebody grab the other oar," he demanded. Nobody moved.

"You wanna die?" he yelled.

Jean-Paul jumped up and grabbed the other oar. As he scanned his side of the boat, he gripped the heavy wooden oar like a giant baseball bat. While Jean-Paul and Murphy were keeping watch on either side of the boat, the two men didn't see the huge shark's monstrous face lunge out of the water from the rear.

"Ahh!" Rachel and Valerie screamed as the shark tried to take a bite out of the boat. Bits of Plexiglas chips and water flew in Muhammad's face. He spit the salty fluid out.

I am so fucked, he thought.

The boat was jerking. The shark's gaping mouth was caught on the metal railing, row upon row of razor sharp teeth sparkling in the sunlight.

"Oh my God!" Sahara screamed.

"Help me Jesus!" Shon prayed.

"Allah, your will be done!" Muhammad whispered.

"We gon' fucking die!" Fame cried.

The boat tipped backwards slightly.

"Oh shit," Wolf yelled, gripping the side.

Murphy and Jean-Paul raced to the back and began beating on the shark's head, while everyone else crawled to the front. The oars were so useless they might as well have been Popsicle sticks. The huge beast jerked its awesome head from side to side.

"Boom!" A gunshot bellowed out of nowhere, blasting through the hot afternoon air like a howitzer. A massive gash opened in the shark's face, splattering blood, bone, and teeth. The shark immediately released its death grip on the lifeboat, twitched for a few moments, then rolled over on its side and floated beside them, dead. The crew was stunned. They looked at Wolf, who was slumped over on his knees gasping for air, both of his hands gripping a .357 snub-nosed Magnum revolver, the barrel still smoking.

"That nigga's got a gun," Fame blurted out. "A *big*-ass gun too."

"You have a gun?" Jean-Paul asked in disbelief. "What in the hell are you doing with that?"

Wolf grinned. "Saving y'all's sorry asses."

Chapter Six

THE STRANDED PASSENGERS stared at each other and at Wolf in disbelief. On one hand they were grateful that he had saved their lives, but they were also thinking, *What was he doing with a gun?* and *What—no, better yet, who—was he going to shoot next?* Fame was the first to speak up.

"Um, look here, man, please don't *shoot me* for asking this," Fame was holding his hands up in a mock surrender. "But what in the hell are you doing with a damn gun *on your vacation?*"

Wolf straightened up, then carefully tucked the huge handgun away in his waistband. He flinched from the still-warm barrel before sitting back against the railing and grinning.

"This here? It's my African-American Express card. I never leave home without it—vacation or otherwise," Wolf said nonchalantly.

"But we're going to a beach party in the Bahamas, not on safari," Fame quipped.

Wolf gave him a stare that said, *Hey funnyman? Shut the fuck up.*

Fame knew that look well and complied. The rest of the survivors sat back down. For the next few minutes they each stole nervous glances at Wolf. He met each and every one of their looks. Clearly, no one was sure what to do next. But after about ten minutes of staring at each other and the endless ocean, their bleak situation came crashing back on them once again. Sammy took it upon himself to break the tension.

" I just realized that we don't even know each other's names."

The rest barely acknowledged his remark. But Sammy would not be deterred. As head legal counsel at David and Sons, a marketing firm based in Washington DC, he was used to running seminars, team meetings, and miscellaneous corporate icebreakers.

Sammy proudly smiled. "I'm Samuel John James and I'm from Washington DC."

"Damn, three first names?" Fame asked. "You must be important."

"Uh, yes, I mean no, hardly," Sammy clarified. "My parents always said that strong names make strong statements."

"Whatever, Thurston Howell," Fame interrupted. "My name is Fame and I'm from Atlanta, and oh yeah, I'm a comedian."

"Comedian? That's what you think," Valerie cracked. "We saw you on BET's *Comic View,* and you ain't all that. 'Fame'? Please!"

"Girl, ain't that the truth," Rachel added, high-fiving her.

Fame sucked his teeth. "Whatever, y'all look familiar too. Didn't I see you two chickenheads getting off Bobby Brown's tour bus?"

Sahara burst out laughing.

The two women cut their eyes at her. Funny thing was, they were both thinking, *How did he know about that?*

Captain Murphy laughed too. "You didn't say where you two were from."

The cousins turned to him. "My name is Valerie Mims and she's Rachel… We're from Houston."

"Sisters?" Jean-Paul asked.

"Cousins," Rachel explained. She looked Jean-Paul up and down. "And where are you from, pretty boy?"

"A town by the name of Lake Charles," he said.

"Louisiana?" Valerie blurted. "That's not that far from Houston. We got kinfolk in Lake Charles. What's yo' last name?"

"Baptiste. My first name is Jean-Paul."

Wolf rolled his eyes. *Fag,* he thought.

"What you all frowned up about?" Valerie asked. "What's yo' name?"

Wolf ignored her.

"Hellooo?" she asked again. "I'm talking to you, DMX."

He cleared his throat. "They call me Wolf, and I'm from Brooklyn."

They should call yo' black ass Wolf-man, Jean-Paul thought.

Wolf looked at Sahara. "And where you from, sweet thang?"

It was her turn to frown. "Don't call me sweet thang. My name is Sahara Hawthorne… I'm from Atlanta."

Shon clapped her hands. "This is just like back at Baptist youth camp! I'm Shon Arrington and I'm from Chicago."

"I'm from Chicago too…my name's Muhammad Jackson."

"Jackson?" Fame couldn't resist. "Why black Muslims be having only half-a-name? Mustafa Green, Osama Bin Lincoln?"

The boat cracked up, even Muhammad.

"Y'all boyfriend and girlfriend?"

"Who, us?" Shon said.

Muhammad cleared his throat. "No, we're co-workers."

Sahara's eyebrow arched skeptically.

Fame's eyes widened. "A Christian and a Muslim on vacation? Does Farrakhan know about that?"

Fame was on a roll. He felt like he was up at the Improv. He turned to Murphy. "And what's your non-boat-driving-ass name?"

Captain Murphy smiled uneasily. "Ethan Murphy—I'm from Hollywood, just outside Miami. And for the record, piloting the boat had nothing to do with what happened. There was some type of explosion."

"Tell that shit to GEICO," Wolf cut him off. He reached over and gave Fame a pound. "Cuz a nigga suing."

"Word," Fame added. "A hundred million."

"I'm like, so hungry," Sahara interrupted, rubbing her flat stomach.

"Oh Lord, don't mention food," Rachel groaned. "I'm starving."

"Girl, I'm thirsty too," Shon said, smacking her dry, cracked lips.

"I hope we don't have to eat each other," Fame quipped. He hungrily scanned the castaways, his eyes resting on Sahara's outstretched thighs. "But then again…"

Sahara flashed icicles in her eyes. "Let's get one thing straight, funnyman. I won't have you or any man on this boat disrespecting me like that. Keep it up and I'ma punch you right in your frog face."

Fame smacked his lips. *Stuck-up ass.*

"That's right, girl," Valerie added. "Cuz, I'll cut a muh'fucka out here."

An enormous belly growl cut them off.

"Sorry," Rachel said, blushing. "I'm just so hungry."

They could all relate. It was their first opportunity to think about anything other than not drowning. They were famished, and just thinking about food was starting to get painful.

Fame grimaced and rubbed his belly too. "Right now, I could go for a big-ass double cheeseburger with some chili cheese fries and an ice-cold Heineken." He paused, then looked at Muhammad and smiled. "Make that a bacon double cheeseburger."

Muhammad ignored him.

"Please y'all stop talking about food," Rachel said.

"There should be something in this lifeboat's chest," Murphy said.

The castaways' eyes flashed wide. Sahara began rummaging through the chest and after a few seconds she shrieked, "There's bottled water in here!"

"Give me one," Wolf said.

"Be careful with that water," Murphy warned. "We need to ration it. We can do without food for a while, but not water."

"There are also a couple cases of MREs," Sahara said.

"What's an MRE?" Valerie asked.

"Meals Ready to Eat," Sammy chimed in. "It's what they serve soldiers in the military."

Jean-Paul laughed. "Yeah, we had them in the Army. They were so nasty we called them Meals Rejected by Ethiopians."

Fame licked his lips and said, "I don't care if they're Somalian shit sandwiches. I'm so hungry I could eat a white girl out."

Some of the men grinned sheepishly while the women rolled their eyes.

Sahara ripped open a case. "Let's see, what do we have here. Chicken à la king. Who wants that?"

"Not me," Jean-Paul winced. He had bad memories of that particular delicacy from Desert Storm, and since there wasn't a restroom on the boat, he knew he'd better pass.

Sahara held the plastic bag up. "Any takers?" She looked at Fame. "What about you, Chris Rock?"

"I'll eat it," he said, reaching out his hand. "Y'all Negroes are crazy. I ain't *never* seen a black person turn down some chicken."

Chapter Seven

"MAYBE THAT CHICKEN À LA KING wasn't such a good idea after all," Fame said, wiping his mouth. The out-of-breath comedian had been hunched over the side of the lifeboat throwing up for the last half-hour.

"Told you," Jean-Paul reminded him.

"T-t-told you my ass, you shoulda *took* it," Fame moaned, clutching his midsection. "I have to take a shit."

"Whoa," Wolf threw his hands up. "You better check that."

Fame was sweating, and his stomach was making audible bubbling noises. "Man look, I'ma hold it as long as I can, but if we don't get rescued soon, this lifeboat is going to be the second boat that gets blown up today."

He wasn't the only one dealing with an upset stomach. Wolf and the Mims cousins were looking more than a little green too. Most of the castaways had fallen asleep rubbing their nervous stomachs. The MREs, combined with the boat's constant rocking, made for a particularly nauseating combination. And the water was getting rougher as the storm moved in, dropping fat raindrops on their sleeping forms. Murphy wiped the rain from his eyes and stared at the dim sky. Not a star in sight. It was hard for him to tell how bad the weather really was since night had fallen. But one thing was certain; the ocean was getting angry. In fact, she was pissed.

"Everybody wake up!" Murphy thundered. "C'mon, wake up, the storm is coming in."

The bleary-eyed and groggy castaways were a mass of confusion. Half of them didn't know where they were; the rest furiously rubbed the sleep out of their eyes.

"Jean-Paul?" Murphy ordered. "Grab those ropes over there. We have to secure everyone to the boat so they won't fall overboard."

Jean-Paul immediately went to work. Sahara helped him unfurl the ropes.

Fame was skeptical. "What if the boat flips over and we're tied to it? We're going down with it. I saw that shit happen in *The Perfect Storm.*"

Murphy was annoyed. "It won't flip over. The storm's not that bad. Besides, if the boat flips we'll probably drown anyway."

"Oh Lord," someone muttered. Others could be heard whispering prayers.

"Uh, thanks...*asshole,*" Fame mumbled.

Four-foot waves began crashing over the side of the lifeboat as the soaked castaways huddled together in the middle of the boat, thinking, *Here we go again.* The swells roared like thunder and the boat sloshed back and forth as though they were in a washing machine set on the spin cycle.

"Ahh! We gon' die," Fame screamed, holding on a lil' too tightly to Sahara's arm. "I'm sick."

"Let go!" she barked, and pushed him off of her.

Muhammad held his hands to the sky. "Allah, Akbar." His prayer made the already nervous crew more nervous. The Mims cousins were silent and sat frozen like zombies.

"Too late to pray," Wolf yelled through the driving rain. "If it's your time to die you can't do anything about it."

Fame frowned. "What if it's *your* time, and we all are just stuck in the boat with ya' ass?" Some of the crew laughed, even Wolf. He had to admit there was logic in the statement.

"Everybody stay calm," Murphy ordered. "We can ride this out. I've been in worse storms."

Chapter Eight

Even though it was drizzling, the party was in full swing inside and outside the Atlantis. Hordes of people were dancing, drinking, and gambling in the hotel's spacious casino. Hardly anyone other than the fleet captains knew that the passengers of *The King's Dream* were missing.

Mike Wilson, though, was nervous. He was sitting at an outdoor bar nursing a drink. He and Jean-Paul had served together in the Army for three years. When they had been stationed in Germany, the two of them had traveled and partied together all over Europe, and they'd kept in close touch with each other since they'd been discharged. Because of his hectic schedule as a local TV news producer, Mike had decided to fly directly to the Bahamas instead of meeting Jean-Paul in Miami.

He should have been here hours ago, Mike thought. *I bet he let Nikki talk him out of coming.*

He glanced at his watch. *Where is the concierge?*

Earlier, Mike had asked the hotel's concierge to contact him at the bar as soon he found out any information. But after an hour of waiting, he decided to go back to his room and check the phone for any messages. As Mike walked into the lobby, an out-of-breath concierge flagged him down.

"Mr., um, Wilson?" the concierge said, pausing to catch his breath. "Sorry, I just came back from the marina. I'm afraid I have bad news about your friend."

Mike frowned. "I knew it. I knew it. He didn't make it."

The concierge looked at the floor. "Sir, no one made it."

"What do you mean?" Mike asked.

"The Coast Guard said the ship must have sunk. They sent a chopper out to look for them and all that was left was a fuel slick."

Mike's eyes flashed. "Huh? Come again."

"The boat is lost, sir. It left Miami but other than that they know nothing."

Mike felt his knees weaken. "But the Coast Guard is still out there searching, right?"

The concierge shook his head. "No, sir. They had to leave because of a storm. I'm sorry, sir."

Stunned, Mike sat down in a nearby chair and sank his face into his hands. *I don't believe it. Jean-Paul is dead?*

Chapter Nine

AFTER THE WIND AND RAIN SUBSIDED, the castaways had their first chance to get some real shuteye. They were exhausted from escaping the sinking yacht and battling the storm. And with the now-calm sea gently rocking their lifeboat, it took no time at all for them to fall fast asleep. The battered little craft was like a giant crib. Their snores nearly drowned out the seagulls. Fame was the first to notice the sun breaking over the horizon and the surprise that it revealed.

"Land! Land!" he screamed, tugging at everyone in sight. "Get ya asses up y'all, there's land!"

"Where?" someone mumbled.

"Over there," Fame pointed at what looked like a mountain off in the distance. "We're saved."

Shon clapped her hands. "Thank you, Jesus."

"Allah be praised," Muhammad smiled.

"Holy shit!" Wolf grinned.

"Told you guys we'd be all right," Captain Murphy said. "Someone grab an oar. Let's row."

"What is this island?" Jean-Paul wondered aloud, picking up an oar.

Captain Murphy scratched his tousled hair and surveyed the island in relation to the sun. "I'd have to say that we must be somewhere in the Out Islands."

"The what islands?" Fame asked.

"There are nearly seven hundred islands in the Bahamas. The Out Islands are at the outer end."

Sammy rubbed the sleep out of his eyes. "Are they inhabited?"

"I hope so," Fame said, rubbing his hands together expectantly. "Maybe they got some half-naked island girls waiting for us on the beach? They might think I'm a god."

Valerie frowned. "Or an ass."

The crew snickered.

Captain Murphy shrugged his shoulders. "Some are inhabited, but most of them aren't."

"What if they're not?" Sahara asked. "What are we going to do?"

Wolf laughed. "I guess we'd be shit out of luck."

Sahara rolled her eyes at him. He winked back.

Half an hour later they were ashore. The beach was brochure-beautiful, and in the fresh morning light, it looked almost as if they'd somehow washed up in Hawaii.

Valerie was the first out of the boat. She excitedly jumped out in the knee-deep crystal-clear water. A few fish scurried out of her way. She splashed around like she was at a water park.

"It's so good to be on land again."

"You ain't lying," Fame cracked as he leapt out of the boat. He hit the beach running like a soldier on D-Day, storming Normandy. "Cuz I gotta *shit*." Once out of the water he kept on running, right into the woods.

"Hey, you better wait," Jean-Paul yelled. "You don't know what's in those woods."

Fame ignored him and kept on running. "I know what's about to *be* in the woods," he yelled over his shoulder.

After the men pulled the lifeboat out of the water, the whole group walked cautiously ashore.

"Thank you, Jesus," Shon said, falling to her knees and kissing the ground.

The island appeared to be heavily wooded, ringed by a wide white-sand beach that extended for what seemed like a few miles. Everyone's eyes darted around nervously for any sign of danger. Wolf had his enormous gun in his hand, which made the castaways even more nervous. Jean-Paul kept one eye on the beach and the other on Wolf.

"Fan out," Jean-Paul said, taking command. "We can cover more beach like that. Me, Sahara, and Captain Murphy will walk over there and check that area out. You guys," he pointed at Wolf, the Mims cousins, Muhammad, and Shon. "You walk that way. Sammy, you stay here with the boat." Everyone started to go his or her way except for Wolf.

"What's the problem?" Jean-Paul asked.

Wolf glared. "Who put you in charge?"

"Quit tripping. I'm the one who was in the military."

Wolf sucked his teeth. "That'd be fine if we were at war. But we ain't."

The Mims cousins were getting antsy. "Why don't you two pull your dicks out and see who got the biggest so we can get on with this," Rachel smirked.

"Fo' real," Valerie added.

"Shut up," Wolf barked. He waved the gun in the air then walked over to Jean-Paul. They were standing face to face. "I got the fucking gun, so *I'm* in charge."

"Oh, Jesus," Sahara mumbled.

"Guys, c'mon," Murphy said, separating them. "We need to stick together. We're all in the same boat here, pardon the pun."

"I agree with the captain," Sammy said. "I think *he* should be in charge. He at least knows the island."

Jean-Paul frowned. Wolf too. "Fuck that," he said, still waving his gun. "He's the one who blew up the damn boat and got us into this mess."

Murphy was indignant. "Yachts just don't blow up. There must have been a leak somewhere." He paused, then looked at Wolf real hard. "Or maybe it was sabotage."

"What the fuck you looking at me for?" Wolf said. "Why would I blow up the boat?"

Captain Murphy paced the shore like a lawyer cross-examining a witness. In this case, a very hostile witness. "Maybe someone was trying to blow *you* up."

There were some confused looks on the faces of the castaways.

"Blow *who* up?" Sahara asked.

"Him." Murphy pointed at Wolf. "Who takes a bodyguard and a gun on vacation?"

"That's ridiculous," Wolf said defensively. "Do I look like a terrorist?"

"The captain does have a point," Sammy chipped in.

"Who cares what you think, Uncle Clarence Thomas?" Muhammad spat out. "You just want the captain in charge because he's white." Shon grabbed Muhammad's hand, hoping to calm him down. He jerked it away.

Sammy puffed out his chest and glowered at him. "I'm not going to be taking too many more of them Uncle Toms."

Muhammad waved him on. "Sorry, would you prefer Uncle Ben?"

That was it. Sammy ran over and tackled Muhammad, who outweighed him by at least thirty pounds. The two men grappled in the sand, legs kicking and hands flailing. Sahara walked over to Wolf and quietly asked him to fire off a round into the air.

"Boom!" went the shot. Everyone froze, including the wannabe gladiators.

"Now that we have your attention," Sahara said. "We're not even on the island fifteen minutes and we're already at each other's throats. If I may offer a suggestion, I think that we all ought to be in charge of something. Captain Murphy, you have the nautical expertise and knowledge of these islands, right?"

He nodded.

"Good, then you should be in charge of getting us off this damn island."

Murphy smiled.

"And you, cowboy," she nodded at Wolf. "Since you have the hardware, you should be in charge of security and, I hope, hunting, if there is any game to be found on this island. So don't waste your bullets. And Jean-Paul—did you have any survival training in the Army?"

"Of course," he said. "I was Airborne."

"Then you should be in charge of helping us *survive*. For instance, where do we get fresh water and shelter?" Even Jean-Paul, though he was still smarting, had to admit Sahara was making some good points.

"I will take care of first aid. Who here can cook?"

Rachel and Valerie raised their hands.

"Good. You two can cook whatever we can find. And you two?" Sahara pointed at Muhammad and Sammy. "Since you have so much energy, go get us some firewood and stuff to build us a shelter."

The group stood there, stunned. Everyone was impressed with Sahara's cool demeanor and logical suggestions.

"Damn," Jean-Paul said with admiration "I think the doctor here should be in charge."

"Aye, aye," Murphy added.

"Like the tribal chief on *Survivor*?" Rachel said. "That's my favorite show!"

They all laughed until Fame came bursting through the bushes, out of breath and in a panic. "Y'all come see. Somebody's living here," he gasped.

Chapter Ten

FOR THE BETTER PART OF THE MORNING, Mike had been in his hotel room summoning the courage to make the call he most dreaded: the one where he told Henri Baptiste, Jean-Paul's father, that Jean-Paul's yacht had gone down. He knew the elder Baptiste very well, having spent many holidays at his large, elegant house in New Orleans.

"Okay, okay, I can do this," he sighed. After punching up the number from his Blackberry's address book, he dialed Henri's house and steeled himself.

Judge Henri Baptiste had just come home after a morning round of golf. He was feeling great, having shot a scorching 79 and handily beating the rest of his foursome, which included the district attorney and two very prominent defense attorneys.

"Who says Tiger is the best black golfer?" he had joked as he pulled his ball out of the eighteenth hole. The fifty-five-year-old widower lived in the tony suburb of Metairie, just outside of New Orleans. He presided over one of the busiest courtrooms in the Crescent City, and rumor had it he was being considered for a spot on the state supreme court. Ever since he'd lost Jean-Paul's mother, Victoria, to cancer three years earlier, Henri had focused on three things: his judgeship, his golf game, and his only son. He was especially looking forward to Jean-Paul's wedding to Nicollete. It was going to be a huge affair. The Baptistes were a large and important family in New Orleans and this was going to be one of the biggest social events of the year.

The wedding would mean the merging of two old and powerful families: the Baptistes and the Richards. For two generations, the Richards had been a major force in Louisiana politics. Nicollete's father, Joseph, was a former United States congressman, and her uncle had been the third black man in state history to run for governor. Many believed that her brother, Robert, was a sure bet to be the city's next mayor. Henri smiled as he placed the morning's scorecard under the magnet on the refrigerator door next to a picture of his beloved Victoria. The phone rang just as he was pouring himself a glass of orange juice. He hoped it wasn't work-related—like some eager detective trying to get a warrant on the weekend. Saturdays were for golf and relaxing, not worrying.

Worry wasn't nearly a strong enough word to describe how he felt when Mike told him what happened.

"Michael, did Jean-Paul put you up to this?" His tone was stern. "If so, tell him this is far from humorous."

Mike swallowed hard. Even delivering good news to the judge made him nervous. This was brutal. "Sir, I wish it was a joke, but his boat never made it to the hotel marina."

"I assume you took the necessary step of checking with the authorities?"

"Yes sir. The Coast Guard sent a helicopter out and all they found was a fuel slick. They said the yacht had sunk."

With that said, the judge's heart also sank, as did all of his dreams for his only son. His knees buckled. Henri groped around for a chair and plopped down. "Did they recover any...any bodies?" he managed to ask.

"N-n-no sir," Mike choked up. He wanted to cry.

Henri was silent. First Victoria and now Jean-Paul. How would he tell Nicollete? The news would crush her. Neither of them had been keen on the idea of Jean-Paul going to the Bahamas for his bachelor party, but what could they do? Jean-Paul was a grown man, and headstrong.

"Sir?" Mike asked.

"Yes," Henri sighed.

"I was thinking of chartering a boat and doing my own search."

The judge perked up. "I don't understand, Michael. Didn't the Coast Guard already conduct a thorough search?"

"Yes, but they had to halt it because of bad weather. And I just feel…it's just a feeling, and I don't want to give anybody false hope, but I just feel like somehow he's still alive out there. I mean, Jean-Paul was Airborne. It would take more than a sinking ship to…um…" his voice trailed off. Mike couldn't bear to say what they were both thinking.

His words gave Henri new strength.

"Michael," he ordered. His voice was booming. "You get what you need. I don't care what it costs. Money is no object. I'm catching the next flight out."

Chapter Eleven

"LOOK, IT'S A HUT," Fame yelled, pointing at a rickety-looking shack. Roughly the size of a two-car garage, the structure looked like a log cabin made out of palm trees. The castaways stared in wonder.

"It's a poachut," Murphy said.

"A poach-what?" Jean-Paul asked.

"A poachut," Murphy said, walking over and inspecting the rickety door. "Poachers, bootleggers, even drug dealers build these shacks on deserted islands and cays so they can offload, transfer, or break down their product before transporting it to the U.S. They're also dump-off points if the Coast Guard chases them."

"You mean they might have some treasure on this island?" Fame asked. Murphy shrugged his shoulders.

"If other people use this island, then it shouldn't take long for one of them to come by and save us, right?" Rachel surmised.

Captain Murphy scratched his head. "Wrong. These are some of the most violent criminals you can imagine. Basically, they're modern-day pirates. They won't help us. In fact, they'd probably kill us to keep us from talking."

Wolf touched the gun in his waistband.

"But this poachut looks really old," Captain Murphy pointed out. "So I doubt we'll be seeing any poachers anytime soon."

"Well, at least we have a shelter," Sahara said. "We should get to work and make this place livable."

"Right," Jean-Paul added. "Guys, let's get some wood. We will definitely need a campfire site." Jean-Paul and Muhammad headed off into the nearby trees to gather wood. As he walked by, Muhammad shot Sammy an evil eye. Murphy took the rest of the men to beach the lifeboat and unload what little supplies they had.

"Make sure to bring the suitcases," Sahara called. She shook her head, still surprised that it had been Fame, out of all of them, who'd had the presence of mind to suggest that they grab a few of their suitcases that had bubbled up to the surface after the ship sank. "Who knows, we might be stranded for a while and you don't want to get rescued and have on dirty drawers," he'd quipped.

Sahara was lucky. One of the suitcases they'd recovered was hers, in addition to Wolf's and Rachel's, but before long they'd all have to share their clothes with the other castaways. As the men went down the shore, the ladies got busy surveying their new house.

"Dang, this floor is hard." Valerie frowned, testing the plywood surface with her foot. "I never slept on the ground before."

Sahara smiled and stared out a makeshift window. She found it hard to believe Valerie's statement. "Don't worry, we'll get some plants and grass and make mats. But we'll definitely be roughing it."

"I hope we won't have to sleep here for long," Shon said. "I have a big project at the office I'm working on."

Rachel smacked her lips. "Girl, later for your project. You better be concerned about getting off this island alive.

"I tell you one thing though," Valerie interjected. "I better get off this damn island before my period, otherwise I'ma turn into superbitch." Her words helped cut the tension and the women all ended up laughing.

Down at the beach, the guys were busy unloading the lifeboat. Murphy was taking a mental inventory of the supplies. Along with the three suitcases and a long plastic tarp, they had three boxes of MREs and four cases of bottled water. Broken down, that meant thirty-six meals and eighty ten-ounce bottles of water. Murphy rubbed his stubbled chin. They would have to ration with care until they found other sources of food and water. Fame, after unloading and opening the first-aid kit, marveled at the contents. "Damn, there's enough stuff in here to do open-heart surgery." It took both arms to lift the aluminum box, and it contained a lot more than Band-Aids.

"Word," Wolf said intrigued. He walked over to inspect the box. "Penicillin, antiseptics…morphine?"

Fame's eyes lit up and he looked closer. "I wonder if they got any cocaine in here," he whispered.

A mischievous grin crossed Wolf's face. "No, but I got some weed," he whispered back, proudly pulling out and unrolling a plastic bag. While Murphy was going through the MREs, he noticed the drugs out of the corner of his eye and shook his head.

"Oh yeah," Fame said, excitedly rubbing his hands together. "Nigga, fire it up."

Wolf frowned. "Shit's wet, son. Gotta dry it out."

Fame studied the partly cloudy sky. "I hope the sun hurry up and come out. I bet they ain't have no chronic on Gilligan's island, huh?"

"Or that fine-ass Sahara either," Wolf added, giving Fame another pound. "I wanna hit that before we get outta here."

"Better not say that around Jean-Paul."

"What, that punk?" Wolf said. "I'll bust his ass."

"Let's start taking take this stuff back," Murphy interrupted. He picked up a couple of cases of MREs. "Fame, make sure you tie the boat to that big stone."

"Aye, aye, Cap'n," he said while giving a mock salute.

Wolf grabbed a case of water and started heading up the hill. Sammy, who had been silent, grabbed two of the suitcases. As Fame bent down to pick up the rope, a sharp ringing came from his pocket. Fame's eyes flashed wide. "Oh shit, it's my cell phone."

"What?" Wolf said dropping the case of water. "Answer that shit."

As he hurriedly fished out the small phone, Captain Murphy and Sammy ran back to them. They all stared excitedly at the phone.

Fame flipped it open. "Hello? Hello? Hello?"

Silence.

Fame took the phone from his ear and looked at the screen as everyone held their breath. Then he let out a yell and heaved the phone far out into the ocean.

"What the hell you do that for?" Wolf asked.

"Fucking low battery alert!"

Chapter Twelve

THE MAGNITUDE OF JEAN-PAUL'S SITUATION was starting to sink in with Mike Wilson. After the storm blew through, the Coast Guard had gone out for another search-and-rescue mission but came back with the same result: no ship and no survivors. They made it clear to him, as gently as they could, that they had plenty of other missions to go on and couldn't devote any more time to what now looked like a lost cause.

To make matters worse, he had also struck out in finding a captain to help him look for his missing friend. It seemed as if there were hundreds of boats in the marina but none were for hire—at least not for a wild-goose-chase rescue mission. He didn't even know where he needed to look. Mike was met with skepticism by most of the boat owners. A few of them seemed to assume he was a smuggler. But the main reason they resisted his inquiries was straight practicality. Nearly all of the boat owners were on pleasure trips, and none of them wanted to risk their expensive ships in the unpredictable waters and weather; it was hurricane season, after all. He'd hoped the yacht company would pay for a salvage crew to raise the sunken ship and get some answers. But the massive expense and time that effort would take made that option unlikely. The company would more than likely just collect its marine insurance and try its luck in court—because there were sure to be lawsuits.

Henri had arrived on the island, but he kept a low profile, especially since he and Mike decided to concentrate on launching their own search-and-rescue mission. But after nearly two days without any takers, things were looking bleak. Also, there was a tropical storm brewing, which had already been christened Henry, which meant one thing: if it was a tropical storm already, then it could become a hurricane soon. As Mike and the judge sat at an outdoor bar strategizing their next move, a tall, slender, dark-skinned man wearing mirrored shades interrupted them.

"Excuse me gentlemen," the man said in a heavy Caribbean accent. "Me uner'stand ya' are looking for a boat captain."

Chapter Thirteen

"Iт's нот аs an alabama cotton field out here," Fame cracked while wiping the sweat from his forehead. He started shuffling his feet and whining, "I bet dey livin' *real* good in da big house."

It was late afternoon and all of the castaways had been sweating bullets all day. It was hot on the island. Alabama hot. Africa hot. There was one lone cluster of clouds floating in the sky like a giant piece of cotton candy. Although the Bahamas have a tropical climate, there isn't a lot of rainfall, which makes for a very dry environment. Even the ever-present sea breeze wasn't enough to ease the heat.

The temperature didn't stop them from working, though. Sahara had taken charge and dispensed orders like a general, though in a milder tone of voice. Privately, she sought advice from Jean-Paul, a real soldier. After Murphy and the other men returned with the supplies, she had them clearing brush and rocks, and marking boundaries for the camp's perimeter. Sammy and Jean-Paul were dispatched to the center of the camp, shirtless and on their hands and knees, digging sand and placing rocks for the group's campfire pit. Muhammad and Shon were put in charge of making beds. These were really "wilderness mats," as Jean-Paul called them. He'd shown them how to line branches side by side and layer grass and plants among them, then cut and place pieces of tarp over them. Inside the hut, the women had cleaned up what would be their living areas. They had fashioned little brooms out of branches and ferns and tied them together with vines. Valerie had also become one of Sahara's first patients on the island after cutting her hand on one of the sharp branches.

"You have any insurance?" Sahara joked.

"Oops—musta left my card at home," Valerie shot back, and cackled.

During a lunch break consisting of MREs and rationed water, Sahara held an impromptu class on the many health hazards of tropical islands. Highest on her list was malaria. Another concern was which poisonous fruits and plants to watch out for. She'd spent a semester in the rainforests of Brazil, and would never forget the time one of her classmates almost died from eating what she'd thought were wild grapes.

But despite all the dangers and uncertainty, there was plenty of beauty all around them, too. They had taken a minitour of the tiny island, walking up and down the beautiful shoreline, splashing in the immaculate waters, and venturing (very carefully) into one of the several caves that dotted the beach. Their noses were also getting attuned to the wonderful tropical smells, like the spicy aromas of Caribbean pine and wild coffee trees, and a host of exotic orchids and other plants. But it was the sounds that affected all of them the most. There are more than 200 different species of birds in the Bahamas, and to the castaways it sounded like at least half of them were on their island. The chirps and squawks of red-legged thrushes and white-crowned pigeons could be heard from deep in the forest, and sometimes not so deep. The occasional grunt of a wild boar sent chills down more than one castaway's spine. As the sun disappeared over the horizon, they wondered what other kinds of animals were in the woods. They were anxious for the campfire to be built, and Jean-Paul—hardened U.S. Army Airborne veteran and, more importantly, former Eagle Scout—didn't disappoint them.

"Damn, Colin Powell, that's a big-ass fire," Fame cracked as he walked up beside Jean-Paul. "What do you plan on cooking, a brontosaurus?"

Jean-Paul poked at the roaring pile of logs with a long stick. "This fire is going to save your scared little ass," he replied.

"I ain't scared," Fame shot back, though all the while his eyes were darting back and forth toward the darkening forest.

As the orange flames licked the growing darkness, Jean-Paul stood back and smiled at his handiwork. Before his discharge five years ago from the Army, he'd often wondered how he could put the many outdoor skills that he'd perfected to use in the outside world. He didn't have many chances to build a campfire in corporate America. One by one the castaways began taking seats around the campfire. Just as if they were schoolkids, they began forming little cliques. Sammy sat by himself, squinting through the darkness at a photo of his girlfriend Lauren. Shon and Muhammad sat with Jean-Paul, Sahara, and Captain Murphy. Fame, who moved in between each group all day, had sat down near Wolf and the Mims cousins. Judging by the pungent smell of marijuana that wafted through the campsite, they were doing more than conversing.

Sahara frowned. "Why don't y'all take that down the beach?"

Wolf grinned. "Don't worry, doc." He held the smoking blunt up in the air. "This here is medical marijuana."

Fame and the cousins giggled. "C'mon chief, we 'round a campfire," Fame added. "Just think of it as a peace pipe."

"Do what you want," Sahara advised. "Your sperm count gets lower with every toke."

"Really?" he said, leering at Rachel. "Low sperm? Maybe I should pass, then?"

"I don't know what your scrawny little black ass is looking at me for," Rachel snapped. The group fell out laughing.

It was around fires like this one that humans first gathered to bond and join together to protect themselves from the dangers of the primitive world. Here people boasted of great feats or told the histories of their clan. While the campfire flickered, the castaways naturally fell into conversations. They told each other bits of their backgrounds and shared brief glimpses of their future plans once they were rescued.

"You know what we need to do?" Fame asked. One by one the castaways turned his way. "We should all get to know each other—really know each other. Who's first?"

They stared at him, stone-faced.

"C'mon y'all, we're going to be here awhile. We might as well get to know each other."

High as a Beverly Hills mortgage, Wolf was leaning back on his elbows looking at Fame through bloodshot eyes. He casually raised a hand.

"Wolf?"

Wolf cleared his cottony throat and looked around at the others. "I want to know how Sammy's black ass pulled that fine-ass white woman."

Fame clutched his sides laughing.

"Her name is Lauren, asshole," Sammy snapped, staring razors at Wolf. Jean-Paul and Sahara gave each other a quick eyebrows-raised look.

Wolf threw his hands up in mock surrender as if to say, *What did I do?*

"I want to know too," Rachel chimed.

"Me three," echoed Valerie.

While most of the rest of them wouldn't have said it, deep down they were all curious.

"I'm with Lauren because she's a sweet and decent human being."

Rachel sucked her teeth and gave her best "sista girl" head twirl. "You sure she ain't with you cuz she thought you had a big Mandingo dick?"

Giggles to outright laughter could be heard around the circle.

"N-no." Sammy struggled to get the word out. "She's not with me because I'm, uh, well hung."

"So little Sammy's got a pencil dick?" Fame cracked, to howls of laughter.

"No, no," Sammy quickly backpedaled. "That's not what I meant."

"Have you met her family?" Muhammad asked in an even voice.

Sammy frowned. "They haven't adjusted to our relationship yet."

"I knew it!" Muhammad snapped. "You can shack up all you want down in the slave quarters, but you better not bring Kunta to the big house."

"Muhammad! That is uncalled for," Shon said. He just looked across the fire at Sammy, his eyes narrow.

Fame turned to Sammy. "And has she met your parents?" He reluctantly nodded his head yes. Sammy felt like he was on trial.

"Why are black people *always* the first ones to accept, and white people *always* have to get *adjusted*?" Fame said. "That's a cop-out way of saying her folks don't want a nigger in the woodshed."

Sammy stood up, wiping the sand off his pants. "You watch your mouth, before *this* nigger kicks your ass."

Fame, who was sitting Indian style, just looked up at him. "Hey, don't get mad at me because her parents are treating you like *the help*. You can come over and meet my parents anytime."

"Aw, man, sit down," Wolf said. "We're just having a healthy discussion."

"Whatever, man," Sammy flicked his hand. "Why don't we have a healthy discussion about how much prison time you served?"

"Ooh," Fame teased.

Wolf's lips creased in a smile that would have made Charles Manson proud.

Rachel interrupted them. "I have a question that I've always wanted an answer to. Why, when a black man gets successful, does he have to get him a white woman?"

It was as silent around the campfire as a mausoleum.

"Yes, Sam-u-el," Fame said, drawing out his name in an exaggerated way. "Can you enlighten us? Inquiring minds want to know."

Sammy ignored him.

"C'mon Sammy, defend yourself, brother," Jean-Paul encouraged.

Sammy rubbed his chin for a moment then blurted out, "Because y'all black bitches won't let a *man* be a goddamn *man*."

"Oh shit!" Wolf and Fame said in unison, laughing. More than a few pairs of eyes bugged out with surprise at Sammy's vehement statement.

"Who you calling a bitch?" Rachel snapped. "You black Sambo looking motherfucker."

"See, that's what I'm talking about," Sammy said. "Y'all so damn aggressive. Always have to show how tough you are. Always running around talking about 'I don't need no man,' knowing *damn well* you need a man."

"Hold up. Wait—" Valerie began to say.

"*Shut up,*" Sammy cut her off. Now that he had the floor he wasn't going to let up. "And y'all so damn lazy. Most of y'all are nothing but welfare moms always trying to get a man to buy this and buy that. Shaking ya ass in the club. Talking about, 'I need a man who look like Denzel and got money like Bill Gates' when all *your* ass is bringing to the table is a piece of *ass.* Black women didn't want me when I was broke and struggling. No, y'all said, Sammy was *too black.* I wasn't pretty enough for y'all." Sammy paused and took a breath while everyone else gaped at him, silent once again, stunned by his rant. Then he held up Lauren's picture, "But this blonde-hair Barbie doll right here, *she* liked this black-assed slave-looking nigga. And that's why I'm with her."

"Whew!" Fame said, finally breaking the silence that followed. "I guess he told *yo* ass."

"Shut up," Valerie said.

Sahara yawned. "On that note, I'm going to sleep." Others stood to follow her into the shack.

"Hold up," Jean-Paul said. "We need to draw straws for guard duty."

"Guard duty?" Muhammad said, surprised.

"Do I look like RamBro?" Fame cracked.

Jean-Paul shook his head. "We don't know what kind of animals are out there in those woods. If we don't have a guard, we might get our asses attacked or eaten."

"He has a point," Sammy said, calmer once again. "Who knows what could be out there? Panthers, pythons..."

Fame cringed. "Oh Lord, did you say pythons?"

Jean-Paul gathered up some small twigs. "We'll draw. Short stick gets first watch. Two hours, then wake the next man. OK?"

"What about them?" Fame said, pointing to the women.

Wolf smacked him upside the head. The ladies smiled as one by one the men picked.

"Fuck!" Fame yelled, grasping a very short twig. He threw the stick into the black forest. "Hey, where you going?" he called after Wolf. "I need to borrow that gun!" Wolf ignored him as he and the rest of the men walked off.

"Don't fall asleep," Jean-Paul yelled over his shoulder.

Pissed off, Fame kicked sand and paced back and forth in front of the fire. He froze with terror each time he heard a hoot or a strange sound coming from the forest. He was still a little high from the marijuana and it made him jumpy and paranoid. He dared not look out into the trees—the branches seemed alive, reaching out to seize his throat. Half an hour later he grabbed a stick and sat down with his back against the doorway of the hut. He looked at his watch and yawned wider than a full-grown lion after a feast. He frowned at the soft sounds of the others sleeping soundly in the shack. He was jealous.

"Guard duty," he mumbled, yawning again. "What is this? Saving Private fucking Ryan?" Within an instant he fell fast asleep.

Chapter Fourteen

EARLIER THAT DAY, back in the Bahamas, Mike and Henri looked at each other cautiously, then turned back toward the mysterious stranger in the mirrored shades.

"How'd you hear that we were looking for a boat?" Mike finally said.

The stranger took off the shades and sat down in the empty chair. "Everyone in da marina knows dat ya looking for a boat." He leaned in closer and whispered, "Even some nefarious characters dat ya don't *wan'* know. You should be more careful."

Henri gave the man a cold look perfected by years of staring down hardened criminals. "How do we know that you aren't one of those, as you said, nefarious characters?"

The stranger's stare was equally icy. "How do I know dat ya not up to no good ya selves?"

Henri was offended. "Sir, I'll have you know that I am judge."

"So? I'm da prime minister of da Bahamas," the man shot back. "Look here, if you wan' play games get ya'selves anudder man. These are treacherous waters ya wan' sail. An' right now I'm ya last chance." The man rose as if to leave.

"Hold up," Mike reached out. "We don't mean any harm. But you have to understand we have reasons to be cautious. We are searching for my friend, who also happens to be his son."

"I une'stand and feel terrible for ya situation, and I assure you dat I come wit' good intentions."

"Okay, let's start over, Henri said grudgingly. "What's your name?"

"Nigel." He reached out and shook each of their hands. "Name's Nigel Benjamin, an' I have ref'rences."

After they introduced themselves, Henri got right to the point. "What kind of boat do you have?" he asked

"I got a great boat, a forty-foot Wildcat. She cuts t'ru da water like hot knife t'ru butta. She very fast."

"What's your price?" Mike asked.

Nigel squinted his eyes and looked at the sky and mumbled something about the weather and the number of islands, then said, "One t'ousand a day."

"A thousand dollars?" Mike asked.

"Plus expenses," Nigel added. "Take it or leave it."

"He's trying to get over," Mike said under his breath to Henri, shaking his head.

Nigel looked at Henri, whose face was a tight-lipped mask.

"OK. You got a deal." Henri shook his hand. "But you better not try and bullshit me. Or someone might have to come searching for *you*."

Nigel wasn't fazed. "Sir, I want to find that ship more than anything in this world, I promise ya dat."

Chapter Fifteen

W HILE FAME SNORED AWAY, a three-foot-long green snake slowly slithered over and then under his outstretched legs before heading into the bushes. Fame didn't move an inch. If it weren't for the elephant-like noises made by his snoring, it was hard to tell he was even still alive. Murphy and Jean-Paul appeared over him, staring down with disgust on their faces.

"Wake your ass up!" Jean-Paul said, kicking Fame's slack body. "Wake your sorry, undependable ass up."

"Huh? What?" Fame jerked awake, mumbling and rubbing the sleep and sand out of his eyes. The rising sun blurred his vision. When he finally managed to focus, he was staring up at two tall figures wearing very sour dispositions.

Fame cracked a smile and attempted to stand. "Ooops. H-hey, guys. Sorry, I must have fallen asleep."

Jean-Paul pushed him back down in the sand. "Sorry? That's all you have to say? You could have gotten us all killed last night." Fame shot a hot glare back at him. One by one, the castaways came out of the hut to see what the commotion was about.

"Jean-Paul's right," Murphy added. "We're very disappointed in you, Fame."

"What's going on out here?" a very sleepy Sahara asked.

"He fell asleep," Jean-Paul explained.

"Look man, I'm a fucking civilian," Fame said, standing up and brushing the sand off of himself. "I don't give a shit about guard duty.

When I'm sleepy, I go to sleep. I said I was sorry. What the fuck do you want from me?"

"We want to be able to depend on you," Murphy said. "It's going to take each one of us helping the others to make it off this island alive."

"Yeah," Jean-Paul said, pointing a finger at Fame. "We all have to pull our weight."

Fame turned and waved an arm at them as he headed toward the woods. "Whatever, man. I'm going to take a piss."

Stunned, Jean-Paul turned to Sahara and Murphy. "Believe this shit? I'm heading down to the boat."

"Forget about Fame," Sahara said to Murphy. "What's the exit plan, Captain?"

"Jean-Paul and I are going to take the boat out and circle the island. Who knows, it might be inhabited, or this might be one of a chain of islands."

"Great id—" she started to say, but was cut off by a very loud yell coming from over the sand dune. The noise came from the same direction that Jean-Paul had headed toward. The castaways scrambled over the dune and froze.

"Fuck! Fuck! Fuck," Jean-Paul was cursing, kicking sand, and flailing his arms in the air.

"What's wrong?" Sahara asked.

"The boat is gone," he yelled.

"Huh? What do you mean?" she asked.

"We left the boat here yesterday," Jean-Paul pointed at the empty beach. "And now it's not here!"

"How could that happen?" Muhammad asked. The group walked down and looked up and down the beach. A few minutes later Fame appeared.

"What's going on? Are we rescued?"

"Fame, did you tie up the boat like I asked you to yesterday?" Murphy asked.

"Tie it to what?" Fame shrugged nonchalantly. "I pushed it up out of the water closer on shore."

"That's it," Murphy said, looking defeated.

"What's it?" Sahara said.

"The high tide came in and the boat went out with it," he said. There were groans and sounds of disbelief from the rest of the group.

"Where did it go?" Rachel asked. "Will it come back?"

Murphy shook his head. "Nope. It's gone. It's floating around out in the ocean somewhere."

They all turned toward Fame. He nervously scratched his chin. Jean-Paul was the first to speak. Better yet, he was the first to yell.

"You mean to tell me that first you fell asleep and now you lost the boat?" He got up in Fame's face and grabbed him by the shirt, growling, "I'ma kick your ass." The other men ran over to break it up.

"Get your hands off me," Jean-Paul said, pushing Wolf's arm away. Outraged, Wolf swung at Jean-Paul, who quickly ducked. The punch missed his face but caught Jean-Paul on his shoulder. He twisted his body and grabbed Wolf and wrestled him down to the ground and started punching him. Fame then jumped on Jean-Paul's back, attempting to break it up, but Sammy saw this and thought that Fame was double-teaming Jean-Paul. He flew into the pile like a middle linebacker. As the men wrestled up a sandstorm, Sahara shook her head in pity. They were like little boys fighting over a ball.

We are never getting off this island, she thought.

"What a bunch of losers," Rachel joked.

"Out-of-shape asses," Valerie snickered.

After nearly three minutes of intense fighting, the guys were exhausted and panting loudly. Fame and Jean-Paul, their faces covered with sand and sweat, were on their knees gasping for air. Meanwhile, Wolf was face down on the beach coughing up sand. Sammy was doubled over with his hands on his knees, sucking in air in deep breaths.

"Are you guys finished?" Sahara asked. "Fighting isn't going to get us off of this island."

The guys were silent. They dusted themselves off and looked at each other. They busted out laughing at how stupid each other looked.

"Y'all negroes couldn't fight a cold," Fame laughed.

Jean-Paul gave a friendly push to the comedian. "I *know* you ain't talking. When you jumped on my back I thought it was a mosquito."

"No doubt," Wolf laughed. "Yo, I thought his little skinny ass was getting ready to Mike Tyson your ear." He then turned to Sammy and looked him up and down before saying, "Damn, nigga, you strong as an ox."

Sammy just smiled proudly.

Sahara wasn't smiling. "Now that you're all buddies again, we still have the problem of how in the hell we are going to get off of this island without a boat."

Fame avoided her icy gaze and sheepishly looked out at the ocean.

"I guess we're going to have to explore the island on foot," Murphy said. "Who's coming?"

Wolf pushed Fame forward. "Here's your first volunteer."

"Oh, no," he whined. "I can't walk too far. I got corns."

"After falling asleep and losing the boat," Jean-Paul cut him off, "You gon' have popped corns if you don't get to steppin'. I'm coming too."

"Me too," Muhammad said.

"Okay," Captain Murphy said. "Grab a bottle of water and let's move out in ten minutes."

Shon touched Sahara's arm. "I got an idea."

"What?"

"Why don't we trace out a S.O.S. on the beach?"

"In case a helicopter or airplane flies by, they can see it?" Rachel chimed in. "Great idea."

While Murphy and the others took off down the beach, the remaining castaways got to work carving out their S.O.S. on the sandy beach.

Chapter Sixteen

Soon, Nigel had taken Mike and Henri way beyond the touristy parts of Paradise Island. The two men gave each other a nervous look as they walked past the row upon row of tin-roofed huts. The sight of what visitors would call a shantytown and its run-down boardwalk so near the island's pristine beach was almost surreal.

"You call *this* a great boat?" Henri asked, pointing at what looked like an obviously unseaworthy vessel. *Queen,* Nigel's forty-foot power-boat, looked instead like it was about forty years old. She was large enough to seat five comfortably. She used to seat eight, but the padding on three of the seats was missing, leaving nothing but rusty springs. The paint had completely peeled off the front of the boat, exposing the white undercoating, which glistened in the afternoon sun like a skinless piece of fried chicken. *Queen* looked like a tired old lady in a rocking chair as she wobbled with the waves.

Nigel ran his hand fondly along his ship's railing, stirring up dusty flecks of rust. "She's top notch. I've sailed all roun' dese islands in her," he lied.

"Looks like it," Mike cracked. He gingerly stepped off the rickety wooden dock and into the boat. "This boat looks like it couldn't sail in a bathtub."

"Look man, me tellin' ya dis a good boat," Nigel said, gesturing. "I'm out in her all da time."

Mike scratched his head. He was unconvinced. "I don't know,

Mr. Baptiste. We go out in this and the Coast Guard might have to come looking for us."

"I agree with you," Henri said.

Nigel stomped his foot down. "I'm telling you, dis a good boat. She got a few miles on her, but I trust her wit' my life."

"I'm just not sure I trust her with mine," the judge said, stepping carefully aboard.

Nigel looked obstinate. "Well, look like ya don't have a choice. Nobody else is goin' ta take ya. Ya wan' save your bwoy?" Nigel slammed his hand down on the dashboard. A small cloud of dust and paint went up in a poof. "Dis is what we ride in."

The judge thought for a moment and then nodded. The thought of his son out there stranded was enough to override his sense of better judgment.

"Okay. When do we get going?"

Nigel smiled. "At dawn. Tomorrow morning."

Chapter Seventeen

JEFF BERARDELLI STARED at the colorful radar loop and sipped from a steaming cup of coffee. It was his third cup of the day. As a senior meteorologist at the National Hurricane Center, it was his job to be alert. Located in Miami, the center's name says it all. The center is responsible for issuing watches, warnings, forecasts, and analysis of hazardous tropical weather. It had already been one of the most active storm seasons on record, and for the past few days Jeff had been keeping a close eye on tropical storm Henry. With winds holding steady at 70 miles per hour Henry was on the verge of becoming a Category 1 hurricane. The storm still had plenty of warm water to churn over, so it was almost a given that it would increase in intensity.

At the moment the forecasted track had Henry heading straight for the Bahamas. Jeff scooted his chair over to a nearby computer to get the latest readout. The weather war room was outfitted with the most advanced satellite technology. From Doppler radar to NEXRAD, the center had all of the tools to plot out the expected track of a storm. Jeff ripped out the printout and mentally crunched the numbers.

"What is this?" he said, doing a double take. "This must be a mistake."

Jeff furiously typed a few keystrokes and reprinted. The printout came out the same. He grabbed the phone and called his supervisor. He looked at to the clock. It was 2:30 p.m. and somehow Henry had now become a Category 2 Hurricane.

Chapter Eighteen

"FAME, YOU BETTER HURRY UP," Jean-Paul yelled into the thick forest. "We're leaving in two minutes." The guys could hear leaves rustling from within the treeline.

"H-h-hold up," Fame grunted. "I'm almost f-finished."

Murphy turned to Jean-Paul and smiled. "I've never seen *anybody* have to relieve himself as much as that guy."

"He's like a baby," Muhammad smirked.

The guys had covered close to seven miles of the shoreline trying to find a way into the island's interior. All they found were a couple of caves, miles of thick forest, and a bunch of bushes. Murphy wiped sweat from his brow and stared at the horizon. "It'll be getting dark soon. Should we be heading back?"

Jean-Paul turned his water bottle upside down and shook it. It was empty. "Yeah, you're right. Let's mo—"

"Ahh!!"

Jean-Paul was cut off by a screaming Fame. He came crashing through the bushes holding the top of his pants together, moving like a blur.

"What the hell?" Murphy blurted out, as the guys jerked their heads in unison.

"Help! Help!" Fame continued to yell, a trail of leaves and twigs flying in his wake. Fresh on his heels were the sharp tusks and thick whiskers of a wild boar. A very *pissed-off* wild boar. Prey and predator were kicking up sand like a dune buggy. The animal was fast, but it was no match for the terrified comedian. As the boar closed in, Fame kicked it into another gear and dove into the surf. Jean-Paul, Murphy, and Muhammad stood there, stunned, as the boar watched Fame slice through the water like a speedboat. The other guys laughed and clapped until the boar turned around, snorting, and headed in their direction. The three men scrambled on top of a nearby boulder. After a minute of huffing, the angry boar, confident that it had established its dominance, trotted back into the bushes.

"That was crazy!" Muhammad said.

Murphy shook his head. "Did you see how fast Fame was running?"

"Like Carl Lewis on crack *and* Red Bull," Jean-Paul laughed.

They jumped down from the boulder and waved the "all clear" sign to Fame, but he continued to dog-paddle about fifty yards offshore.

Meanwhile, back at the camp, the rest of the castaways had finished making their S.O.S. As Sahara stood atop a sand dune admiring their handiwork, Wolf eased up beside her.

"Looks good, huh?" he said.

She wiped the sand off her hands and put them on her curvaceous hips. "Yes. I'd have to agree."

"But not as good as you look in those capris," he whispered.

Sahara frowned at him. "Don't even go there. You're not my type."

Wolf sucked his teeth. "Yeah, I know what type your stuck-up ass likes."

Her eyes flashed angrily. "Don't worry 'bout what I like. It's none of your business," she said, and turned to walk away. Wolf grabbed her arm—firmly, but not too tight. She angrily jerked it away. He smiled.

"Remember this, sweet-thang," he said as she walked away. "A lot can happen before we get off this island."

Chapter Nineteen

BY THE TIME JEAN-PAUL and the other guys returned, the camp-fire was roaring again. Dusty and haggard after walking nearly fourteen miles, they looked like soldiers coming home from a battle. Fame collapsed in a heap.

"Look at him," Rachel said. "What happened?"

"You don't even want to know," Jean-Paul mumbled, accepting a bottle of water from Sahara. Leaning back against a tree, Wolf made silent note of their exchange.

"I almost got killed!" Fame blurted.

Murphy and Muhammad shared a knowing smirk.

"Go ahead and laugh," Fame said. "A big-ass elephant or saber tooth or something damn near stabbed me to death. I had to jump in the damn ocean to get away from it." He reached out to Rachel. "I need a hug."

She pushed his hands away. "You better hug yourself."

"It wasn't an elephant. It was a wild pig, " Jean-Paul corrected Fame. "And you should have seen his ass hit the water. I thought he was going to hydroplane all the way back to Miami."

The castaways laughed—all except Fame.

"A pig?" Wolf said, rubbing his stomach. "Why didn't y'all kill it? We coulda had a luau."

Everyone laughed at this.

"Besides running with the pigs, did you guys see anything?" Sammy asked.

"No," Jean-Paul said. "We just walked up the shore. We tried to cut through the interior, but without a machete, it was useless."

"Tomorrow we'll head the other way or try to go through there," Murphy said, pointing in the direction of the trail they had carved heading toward their makeshift latrine.

"Count me out, Cap'n," Fame said. "After guard duty and that Army road march, I need some combat pay."

"I'll take his place," Sahara volunteered.

"Good," Jean-Paul said.

"Me too," Sammy said.

Jean-Paul looked at Wolf. "What about you, Wolf?"

He was curt. "I don't think so, Sarge. But maybe me and Fame will go hunting for some wild pig," he added, smiling.

Fame gave him the finger.

While the castaways relaxed around the fire, Wolf lit up a blunt.

"Oh goodness," Sahara sneered. "There you go again."

"Why are you always beefing about my weed?"

"Because it's bad for you."

"Is it worse than a boat exploding and leaving my black ass stranded on a deserted island?"

"He got a point," Fame interjected.

"You mean to tell me you've never gotten high before?" Wolf asked.

Sahara shook her head no.

"Ever gotten drunk?"

"Nope."

"What about you?" Wolf pointed at Muhammad.

"I don't pollute my body with that filth," he said, frowning.

Wolf ignored him and held the blunt in the air. "Anybody want a hit?"

Shon blinked and said, "I get high off Jesus."

Wolf snickered, "Jesus ain't never had no chronic like this."

"Jesus drank wine, and he had the bangin' ass fish fries," Fame snapped. "If that don't prove he was black, nothing will."

Wolf held out the smoldering blunt to Jean-Paul. He waved him off.

"Nerd."

"But I got all my sperm, nigga," Jean-Paul shot back.

Wolf extended the smoking blunt to Captain Murphy. Murphy looked at the other castaways and grinned.

"I knew it!" Wolf cackled. "You a white boy and y'all love to get high. Y'all be eating mushrooms and shit." He handed the blunt to the captain. Murphy hesitated. The castaways looked at him to see what he was going to do.

In fact, Murphy was very familiar with drugs. He had gotten high the very night before their ill-fated cruise. As the pungent aroma from the marijuana floated in the air around them, he took a deep breath and accepted the blunt from Wolf. As everyone watched, he took a long pull, held it for several moments, then blew an expert stream of smoke from his nostrils.

"Our captain is a crackhead," Fame cracked. A few of the castaways snickered.

"Ha! Ha!" Wolf said. "That's that 'danebrammage.'"

"Huh? Danebraine? What?" Murphy asked. "What do you call it?"

Wolf laughed. "This weed is so good you can't even say brain damage. Who's next?"

"I am," Sammy said, reaching for the blunt.

Wolf damn near broke his neck. "What?"

Fame raised his head like an English setter. "Sammy smokes? Aw! Shit! I knew you were a playa! An Oreo playa! But a playa nonetheless."

"Damn, this is some good marijuana," Sammy said. "My compliments to you, Mr. Wolf."

"Compliments?" Wolf said, confused.

"Forgive me," Sammy apologized. "Reefer tends to bring out the aristocrat in me."

That cracked up all of the castaways. Next Rachel, then Valerie and Fame all took hits from the blunt and passed it around. Moments later they were sprawled out around the campfire glassy-eyed.

Sahara shook her head in disgust. "Y'all a bunch of fiends."

Fame held up the half-smoked blunt. "Doc, we *are* gon' get your pretty ass high before we get off this island."

Jean-Paul leaned back against a tree and began plucking leaves off a twig. "Guns and drugs on a deserted island? What else you got in your bag of tricks, Wolf? Hookers?"

"Already taken care of," Wolf smiled, looking in the direction of Valerie and Rachel, who were busy sharing the last of the blunt.

Valerie ignored him. She was used to men like him making those kinds of remarks.

"Can I ask you a question?" Sahara said to Wolf.

"Sweetheart, you can ask me anything."

"What do you do for a living?"

It got real quiet around the campfire. It was a question all of them had considered but were too scared to ask. Wolf rubbed the stubble on his chin for a few seconds. With no razors in sight, nearly all of the men had at least five o'clock shadows.

"I'm a drug dealer," he said flatly.

"Now that's breaking news!" Sammy blurted out. The group all laughed at his sarcasm.

A confused look crossed Rachel's face. "I thought you told me you were a pharmacist."

"A *street* pharmacist," Fame cut her off. The castaways howled with laughter. Even Wolf found it funny.

"I can't believe you just admitted that," Sahara said.

"Why not?" Wolf shrugged. "Y'all don't know me or where I live." His eyes then became cold and hard. "Besides, I'd kill any of you if you snitched to the cops, so remember that."

Once again, silence fell over the group.

"Well, that just killed my buzz," Valerie sighed.

Muhammad was indignant. "How can you sell that poison to your own people? In your own community?"

"Yeah," Jean-Paul echoed.

"Easy," Wolf said. "It's called m-o-n-e-y."

Muhammad spit in the sand. "But damn, black man. That shit is killing us."

Wolf was unfazed. "Black man, my black ass. Don't put that on me. We're killing ourselves. If I don't sell it to them, somebody else will."

"That's a cop-out," Jean-Paul said. "Why not be part of the solution instead of the problem? That's the only way we gon' win the drug war."

"You sound like one of those sappy-ass public-service announcements," Wolf snapped. "Listen here—I'ma school you on the drug trade. First of all, it ain't like I'm flying the shit into the country. I got money, but I ain't got no fuckin' planes. I get my weight from a white boy who gets his from a Colombian. Shit goes through customs, diplomatic channels, the feds, the police. And you better believe *they* all get a cut. It don't matter if I stop—the *drugs* ain't gon' stop.

"And it ain't just crackheads doing crack," he continued, sounding more serious and earnest than he had before. "I ain't selling to any poor pregnant mothers and defenseless school kids. My portfolio is diversified. You should see all the rich yuppies I sell to—shooting up my heroin all night and trading stocks all day. Oh, and you can't forget my soccer moms, who like to snort a few lines to get through the day." Wolf's sinister grin was back, and he turned it toward Sahara. "And don't get me started on all the doctors who smoke a gang of weed to get through the stress of surgery—and they ain't smoking no medical marijuana either."

"Whatever," Sahara said, frowning.

Wolf continued. "It's all interwoven. Y'all naive if you think that America is *ever* going to win the drug war. First of all, do you know how many people that would put out of a job? On both sides of the law? Not to mention how those drug treatment centers won't be able to stash that government grant money anymore. And do you know how much laundered cash flows though our economy? Shit would wreck Wall Street."

Sahara had a sad look on her face. "It's just a business to you, huh?"

"Baby, it's always business."

Chapter Twenty

NIGEL GUZZLED THE LAST SWIG from his Red Stripe and checked his gauges. He cranked the engine, which didn't catch, while nonchalantly crushing the can and then throwing it into the back of the boat. The crumpled can landed on top of a small pile of other crumpled cans. He let out a foghorn-like belch. Mike stared at him in amazement.

"You sure you're going to be okay driving this thing?" he asked, his right eyebrow arching cautiously.

"Course," Nigel said, and burped again. "Don't worry, I could pilot her while I sleep."

"That's what I'm afraid of," Mike mumbled. "Hey, what happened to your accent?"

Nigel ignored him.

Mike loaded the last of their gear into the boat. Nigel had told him and Henri to plan to be out all day, so they had packed plenty of water and food. All Nigel had packed, apparently, was Red Stripe.

Mike smacked his lips. His throat was dry, and even though it was eight o'clock in the morning, a cold beer didn't seem like such a bad idea. "Can I get one of those?"

"Course," Nigel said again, smiling broadly. "You don' have ta ask."

Mike walked over to a big red ice chest that sat in the front of the boat. Out of the corner of his eye, Nigel noticed him reach down to open it.

"Hold on! Dat's not it, mon," he yelled. Nigel nearly broke his neck jumping over a stack of gear to shut the ice chest. He bent down and snapped it shut.

Mike backed up, slowly raising his hands. "Uh, okay, bruh," he said, slightly thrown off. "Didn't know that you had nuclear secrets in there."

"No secrets, mon, no secrets. Just, you know, navigation equipment," Nigel said, looking away as he returned to his spot behind the wheel.

"Sure, whatever," Mike said, not believing a word of it.

Moments later Nigel cranked the starter again. The old engine sounded like a horse whinnying. Henri leaned back uneasily in a tattered seat belowdecks and listened.

"Dear Lord, watch over us today," he silently prayed while he double-checked the fasteners on his life preserver. After few more loud cranks of the ignition, *Queen* screeched to life and slowly peeled itself away from the boardwalk as if she were duck-taped to the dock. Mike shot a cautious glance at the smiling Nigel. He knew that in no time at all the boat would be slicing through the water. Minutes later, she was. Mike had to admit that the boat did ride the waves nicely. Maybe *Queen* wasn't such a sorry tub after all.

Nigel gunned her in a northwestwardly direction. The first place he went was the last known coordinates of *The King's Dream*. Henri had secured that particular piece of information only after a heated discussion with the Coast Guard and a quick call to some very high-placed friends in Washington. Both Henri and Mike agreed with Nigel that the best thing for them to do was to start there and then search the nearest islands. He got them to the coordinates in little more than an hour. Once there, Nigel idled the boat while the other men stood on the deck and silently peered off into different directions. Henri was lost in thought as he fought back tears.

"Hang on Jean-Paul, I'm coming for you," he whispered to the wind.

"So Nigel," Mike asked, while staring at the expanse of ocean, "Which way now?"

Nigel unfolded a tattered map on the large console. The map was so torn and discolored it looked like it could have belonged to Columbus. "Dis way," he said pointing at a massive chain of islands. The three men stared at the map.

Mike pointed at a long scattered string of islands. "What's that?"

Nigel frowned. "It's da Bahamas."

"Huh?"

"We just came from the Bahamas," Mike said.

"Da Bahamas is a big place, mon," Nigel explained. "There are nearly a t'ousand islands in da whole chain."

"Whoa. Really?" Mike said. Henri too seemed surprised.

"Yes," Nigel pointed at the farthest tip of the map. "And we're going ta start over here."

"What's that area called?" Henri asked.

"Da Out Islands," Nigel smiled.

Henri squinted at the map. "The Out Islands, huh? Looks like there could be a million places for a boat to land."

"There are," Nigel confirmed.

"Are you familiar with these islands?" Henri asked.

The captain turned the ignition. This time *Queen* purred to life on the first try. Nigel swerved her in a half-donut spin, spraying a plume of fresh ocean in her wake.

"I know dese coves and cays like a smuggler."

I'll bet, Mike thought.

Chapter Twenty-One

 IT WAS JUST AFTER SEVEN O'CLOCK the next morning when some of the castaways convened outside the hut to plan their next excursion. This time the group consisted of Jean-Paul, Sahara, Murphy, and Sammy. They were in good spirits. It looked like a promising day for a walk. The beach was glittering in the bright morning sun and the weather was a comfortable 75 degrees, Jean-Paul estimated, without a cloud in sight.

Jean-Paul spread his arms to take it all in and sighed happily, adding, "Tourists pay thousands of dollars to wake up to tropical mornings like this. This is the kind of day that makes you wish you never had to go back home to a nine-to-five."

Sahara smirked. "And just think, we're getting it for free." She turned to Murphy and asked, "So Cap'n, which way do we go?"

"I figure we head a few miles that way this time. We have to see something," he said, pointing down the beach.

Sahara squinted her eyes in that direction. "How do you figure?"

Murphy shaded his eyes and pointed to direct Sahara's gaze. "The shoreline curves, there, and look at those birds circling in the distance."

"Could be vultures," Sammy said grimly.

Sahara lightly flailed her arm at him. "Don't say that," she chastised him.

"I got something for them," Jean-Paul said confidently. He was gripping a makeshift club that he'd fashioned out of a sturdy tree branch.

"Who are you, Captain Caveman?" Sahara teased.

He winked his eye and puffed out his chest. "Just call me Captain Afro-America." Just then, Fame emerged from the hut. Jean-Paul turned and asked, "Hey tough guy, sure you don't want to come?"

"Hellll nooo," Fame got out through a huge yawn. "Y'all look like you just got voted off the island." They waved him off and started down the shore. Once they'd all turned away, Fame shook his head pitifully and rubbed his belly.

I need to take a shit, he thought, before once more heading off into the woods. He nearly bumped into Rachel, who was carrying a couple of water bottles with her.

"Where you going, sexy?" Fame leered.

"Boy, shut up," she snapped.

"Oh, gotta take a dump too, huh?"

"No, fool, I'm going to wash up," she growled, before turning to walk off into the woods.

"With that water?" Fame asked. "We need that to drink."

Rachel frowned. "This ain't drinking water. This is rainwater."

"More like acid rainwater. Better watch out, might make your titties fall off."

"Whatever, you should try some."

Fame rolled his eyes. "Shit, I ain't took a bath since we been here."

As Rachel stomped off, she threw out, "I can tell, cuz I can smell."

As Fame and Rachel walked off in separate directions, Wolf quietly emerged from the hut. He tiptoed so as not to wake up the remaining castaways. He'd overheard the whole conversation between Fame and Rachel. Wolf smoothed his gun where he'd sat it in his waistband. He let Rachel get a few minutes' head start before he slowly and stealthily followed her.

Rachel had found a very small clearing about fifty yards from the hut. The plants and surrounding trees were thick. It was eerily quiet except for the persistent chirping of birds.

I hope there ain't any monkeys on this island, she thought, nervously scanning the trees. Rachel had been irrationally terrified of monkeys since she and Valerie were little girls. She undressed and began pouring water all over her ample chest and stomach.

"Whew!" she exhaled, flinching. *Dang, that's cold.*

As she rubbed her hands all over her body Rachel was unaware that she was being watched. Standing behind a thick growth of plants, Wolf peered through the leaves like a prowling lion stalking an unsuspecting antelope. Tiny beads of sweat trickled down his forehead. He licked his lips and his breathing became heavy.

"You missed a spot," Wolf growled. His voice was low and evil.

Rachel froze. Her heart raced. She tried to scream but her voice abandoned her. Terrified, she reached for her clothes.

"You won't be needing those," Wolf whispered.

"Who is that?" Rachel managed to ask.

"Hello, Little Red Riding Hood, it's the big, and very bad Wolf," he smirked, pushing his way toward her through the undergrowth.

"Boy, w-w-what you doing here?" Rachel asked, while feverishly pulling on her shirt. Her eyes never left Wolf. He began slowly walking toward her. Rachel backed away cautiously. "No, Wolf, please don't."

He raised his finger to his lip. "Shush."

"I'll scream," she threatened, a rush of boldness overcoming her.

Wolf raised his shirt, revealing the butt of the gun. "No you won't."

Rachel backed away faster but tripped over a rock and fell flat on her back. An instant later Wolf stood over her. Raw terror filled Rachel's eyes. She started sobbing. "Oh God, please, I'm begging you."

Wolf smiled. He loved it when they begged. And they always begged. He pulled out the gun. His grip was tight as he pointed it at her. Rachel whimpered like an injured puppy.

"On your knees," he commanded. She hadn't had time to button her shirt, and her full breasts were exposed as she kneeled in front of him. Tears began to form in her eyes as Wolf slowly pressed the gun against her heart. It beat like African drums. Rachel closed her eyes and prayed for a quick death. Wolf then began using the barrel of the gun to trace imaginary circles around her breasts, then down to her crotch.

"How does that feel?" he said, squeezing his bulge. "It feels good, huh?"

From somewhere deep down, Rachel summoned all her courage. She just stared defiantly up at him through her tears. Wolf's lips curled into a menacing frown. He grabbed her by the throat and put the gun to her lips. She winced, and her courage began to evaporate by the second. His face was inches from hers. Wolf's teeth were a nasty shade of yellow and his morning breath was hot and very funky. He stuck his long tongue out and licked her tears.

"Open your mouth, bitch," he ordered. As Rachel's full lips parted, he slowly slid the barrel inside her mouth. A stream of piss trickled down her legs.

"Don't you know I will blow your motherfucking head off?"

Rachel nodded.

He then kissed her cheek and whispered, "Now, we are going to do what I say, right?"

Rachel nodded again.

"That's good." He released his grip on her throat and she fell back gasping for air. "Now unzip my pants."

After she had nervously unzipped him, Wolf pointed the gun to her forehead. "Now, suck my dick like your life depends on it."

Chapter Twenty-Two

"CAN WE TAKE A BREAK?" Sahara asked, a bit winded and sweaty. She used her hand to shield her eyes from the blazing glare and to take in the beauty of the waves breaking onto the shore. She felt like walking right into the cool waters. What had started out as a nice walk along the beach was fast becoming a military march.

Jean-Paul wiped sweat from his forehead and smirked. "A break? We've only been walking for a couple of hours."

"More like four," Sahara countered, glancing at her watch. "Forgive me. I didn't go to Ranger School. I'm tired and I'm hungry."

"And I'm thirsty," Sammy said, smacking his dry and cracked lips. He then kicked off his sandals and plopped down Indian-style in the hot sand and proceeded to rub his aching feet. "My dogs are barking. Feels like we've been walking around in circles."

They all turned to Murphy, who was about ten yards away. He was staring at the sky. "I think that's because we have been."

"What?" the group said in unison. Jean-Paul quick-stepped over to him. "We've been walking in a circle?"

Murphy shrugged. "Not a complete circle, but if I'm right, in a few more miles we'll be back at camp."

"I'll be damned," Jean-Paul mumbled.

"Geez!" Sahara shouted. "What do we do now?"

"We can explore the interior of the island," Murphy said, trying to give them some hope.

Sammy shook his head. "That's straight-up jungle. I'm not going in there," he said flatly.

"More importantly, how is going in there," Sahara added, pointing into the thick growth, "going to get us off of this island?"

"Maybe there's water. I know there is definitely food in there," Jean-Paul said.

Sahara walked over and patted him on the back. "Good luck, Mr. Hunter. I'm a gatherer, as in gathering firewood to cook what you bring back from the hunt."

Jean-Paul looked at the guys and held up his hands as if to ask, "Fellas can I get some help?" He got none.

"Speaking of food—c'mon man, break out those Meals Rejected by Ethiopians," Sammy said.

"Sure you don't want to walk these last few miles into camp?" Murphy asked. They looked at him like he'd just clubbed a baby seal.

"Food!" Sahara ordered.

Jean-Paul obliged, rummaging through the makeshift knapsack, which was really just a shirt with the sleeves twisted into a knot. "What do we have here? Ah, chicken à la king." A collective groan rippled through the castaways. "No takers, huh?"

To say they were hungry would have been an understatement. They tore through the MREs like wild animals.

Sammy was smacking a mile a minute. "I think I'm starting to, uh, *brrp!* excuse me, enjoy these dehydrated pork patties. How do they keep the spaghetti and the bread so fresh?" he added, licking his fingers.

"I hate to say it, but this chicken and rice tastes like Emeril made it," Sahara cracked, wiping a few loose grains of rice off of her lips. "But I'll tell you—I'd never eat this crap back home."

Jean-Paul smiled. "If you were in the Army, you would have. In Kuwait, this was all we ate for nearly a year."

"I don't how you did it for an entire year," Sammy said, rubbing his now-bubbling stomach. "These things give me horrible gas."

"How long were you in the Army?" Captain Murphy asked, opening up his bag of tuna and noodles.

Not wanting to talk with his mouth full, Jean-Paul held up four fingers.

Sahara's eyes blinked wide. "Four years?"

"No, four-ever," Jean-Paul joked.

"Why did you get out?" Sammy asked.

"My father."

The group looked confused.

"Well see, my father has this thing about the men in our family. We all have to go into the Army for at least a couple of years, so we can learn discipline and responsibility."

"Did you?" Sahara asked.

"I guess so. But I also learned the fine art and ancient techniques of being a wino."

"I know what you mean," Captain Murphy laughed. "Before I went into the Navy, I was a teetotaler. After six months on a destroyer, I was damn near an alcoholic."

Jean-Paul nodded. "Tell me about it. If we weren't on maneuvers, we'd be in the barracks or NCO club tossing back shots."

"My father wouldn't let my brother go into the military," Sahara said. "He said, 'The Army is no place for a black man.' Too much racism."

"I totally disagree," Murphy said, his voice rising. "I was on a destroyer in the Persian Gulf during Desert Storm, and we had a lot of blacks on board. There weren't any problems."

Sahara smiled and said, "I bet some of your best friends were black, huh? What about all those reports of poor blacks and Latinos on the front lines?"

Sammy frowned. "What's wrong with serving your country? My grandfather was a sergeant major. He fought in Korea."

"Nothing's wrong with it—if you're white," Sahara said sarcastically.

Jean-Paul shrugged. "The military is like any other part of society. It has its pros and cons. It's what you make of it. But I ain't gonna lie, it was tough. I had three white roommates when I graduated from basic training. One was a hillbilly from the mountains of West Virginia who said he had never seen a black man 'til he went into the Army."

"Really?" Sammy asked, looking skeptical.

"Another was from Texas. His father was a Ku Klux Klan Grand Wizard or some shit like that back home. And the last one was from New York City."

"Well, at least they weren't all rednecks," Murphy said.

"Right," Jean-Paul grinned. "The New Yorker was a skinhead neo-Nazi devil-worshiper."

They all laughed except Sahara, who asked, "Whoa. How did you deal with that?"

"Well, the first thing I told them was that they had to take down that Confederate flag, get rid of the Nazi storm trooper helmet sitting on the shelf, and throw out that damn satanic bible."

"A satanic bible? What did they do?" Sammy asked, wide-eyed.

In an exaggerated southern drawl, Jean-Paul said, "The Texan said, 'Look here nigger, we ain't takin' nuffin' down off a dat der wall."

"No they didn't?" Sahara gasped.

Jean-Paul nodded his head yes.

"Did you report them?" Sammy asked.

"Wouldn't have done any good. I was a private, fresh out of basic, lowest of the low."

"Well, what did you do?" Captain Murphy asked.

"Well, after I called them all kinds of cracker-assed crackers, I went out and bought a big poster of Malcolm X and some Minister Farrakhan Nation of Islam tapes, then borrowed a controversial book from one of the more radical brothers in the barracks that I displayed on the nightstand."

"What was the book?" Sahara said.

"*The White Man Is the Devil,*" Jean-Paul deadpanned.

They all roared with laughter.

"And you know what? After a few months of serious and intensive debates about race, we all became kind of close."

"That's twisted," Sahara said.

"Society is sick and twisted," Jean-Paul offered. "But I loved my military experience."

"So why did you get out?" Sahara asked.

"Oh, like I said earlier, my father. He's a judge in New Orleans and he's into politics. Once I had my head screwed on straight, he wanted me to come back to college, then law school, then to marry the daughter of one of his cronies, have some damn kids, and get into politics."

"You're a lawyer?" Sammy asked.

"Unfortunately."

"Why do you say that?" Sahara asked

"It's what he wants me to do, not what I want to do."

"What do you want to do?" Sahara pressed.

"I want to be a writer."

Sahara stared at him intently. "You never said you were married."

He looked away. "I'm not—yet. I'm engaged."

"Engaged. Really?" she added.

"Y-yeah," Jean-Paul stuttered. "But, uh, I don't think I'm ready. Nikki," he added, coughing slightly as he said her name, "that's my fianceé's name, she's ready to have a bunch of kids and I'm just not ready for that."

"You don't like kids?" Sahara asked, eyebrows slowly arching.

"No, I mean, uh, yes." Jean-Paul felt like he was on the witness stand. He wished he'd never opened his mouth. "Whoa, look at the time. We should head back to camp."

"Yeah. Let's," Sahara mumbled.

Chapter Twenty-Three

NIGEL WAS FINISHING HIS FOURTH RED STRIPE and there was still no sign of the Out Islands. After tossing the crumpled can to the wind, he noticed something sparkling off in the distance, like a mirror reflecting sunlight. He pushed back his cap and scratched his head, his mind racing. Nigel knew he had to act fast. Mike and Henri sat below deck, sleepy and very hot. The boat's speed created a constant breeze, but it was still a hot breeze, like an electric fan blowing in hell. With the sun close to its blazing peak, the cramped quarters below deck made the *Queen* feel like the *Amistad*. Suddenly they were jolted back to full consciousness by a sudden swerve. Dazed, Mike wondered if they had hit an iceberg. As he reached for the wall to gain his balance, he realized Nigel was making a very hard right turn. A number of books and knickknacks lining the shelves flew all over the floor, and Mike fell squarely in Henri's lap.

"Get up off of me," the judge said, pushing him away while looking up the stairs. "What in the name of all that's good and holy is he doing up there?"

The two cautiously climbed back up above deck only to find Nigel looking nervous and gunning the engine. As the *Queen* increased in speed, it crashed violently through the seas. Mike and Henri had to grip the railing and each other to keep from falling overboard.

"What are you... doing?" Mike yelled as the wind sliced his words into little muffled wisps. Nigel waved him off.

"Get back down, mon," he ordered.

Henri was indignant. He slowly made his way over to Nigel. "I will…not," he managed to bellow in between breaths. "Not…until you tell me…what in the devil you are racing for."

Nigel's mind was a gumbo of thoughts. He dug deep, stirred, and quickly scooped out an answer. "Uh, land, up ahead."

Henri and Mike squinted and looked all around. All they saw was an endless expanse of water. "I don't see anything," Mike said. The judge nodded in agreement.

Looking in no particular direction, Nigel lied. "Dat way." He was getting irritated. "Trust me, get back down. Me want ta' get dere 'fore it gets too dark."

Unconvinced, Mike and Henri surveyed the distance one more time before stumbling back below deck.

"I didn't see anything," the judge whispered. "I think he's up to something."

"Me too," Mike agreed. "We better keep a close eye on him."

They weren't the only ones keeping a close eye on Nigel. If they would have squinted a little harder in the distance they might have seen the bow of a ship pursuing them. Nigel had instantly recognized the glint of a mast in the sunlight along with the unmistakable outline of a flag. It was a sight he was more than familiar with. It was a United States Coast Guard cutter, named *Jesse Owens*. The name of this ship always made Nigel smile to himself, however grimly, because it was notoriously slow. Still, it was the Coast Guard—and it looked like it was coming after him

Damn, he thought, looking at the red cooler. *I should dump it overboard*. No, he shook his head. The Coast Guard could put an end to his freedom, but if he didn't deliver the contents of that cooler, Nigel was sure to end up sleeping with the fishes. *Maybe they hadn't spotted us?* Taking no chances, he pushed the throttle forward to fifty knots. *Queen* vibrated a bit but held steady. She was really a converted "go-fast" boat, a favorite of "super smugglers"—a group of which Nigel was a charter member. A boat like this was not easily detected by normal radar. Nigel must have stumbled into a routine patrol. His only hope was to get to one of the secluded cays of the Out Islands.

The Caribbean has long been a smuggling route. South American cocaine cartels use many of the hundreds of islands, along with Haiti, Puerto Rico, and the Dominican Republic, as staging points from which they move millions of tons of drugs into the United States. Some even go so far as using submarines. But as the smugglers have gotten more sophisticated, so has law enforcement. One of the best weapons in the war on drugs was the "Famous" class of Coast Guard cutters like *Jesse Owens*. At 270 feet long and weighing 1,800 tons, these ships are outfitted with the latest high-tech surveillance equipment, as well as weapons like the MK 75–76mm deck gun and twin .50 caliber machine guns. Enough firepower to give Dirty Harry a hard on. The *Jesse Owens* was also equipped with the Hitron MH-68A helicopter, better known as the *Shark*. The cutter might be slow, but there isn't a boat made that can outrun the Hitron's 140-knot cruising speed or its on-board sharpshooter. Once the *Shark* gets near a fleeing vessel, the sharpshooter fires a warning shot across the bow with a machine gun. If the boat doesn't stop, next to come out is a specially designed net, more like a giant spiders' web, that's used to entangle the boat. The combination of the cutter and the helicopter has been a major reason why the Coast Guard has been able to seize nearly a million pounds of cocaine and half a million pounds of marijuana in Caribbean waters since 1998.

As Nigel kept *Queen* near its top velocity, the *Jesse Owens* slowly but surely faded from sight, just as the first of the Out Islands came into Nigel's view.

"Yes," he said, triumphantly pumping his fist in the air. "We home free."

That's when Nigel looked behind him and spotted what looked like a giant dragonfly on the horizon.

Chapter Twenty-Four

OH SHIT! Nigel thought, nearly panicking. He had no doubt about what was on his tail. The *Shark* was less than a few hundred yards away and was eating up the remaining distance by the second. Nigel's hands gripped the steering wheel so tight his knuckles glowed white. *Think, think of something! Five minutes, that's all I need to get to that island.*

It was time for evasive action. Nigel waited until the *Shark* was within a hundred yards from him and then he jerked the steering wheel, zig-zagging hard to the left and then to the right. Seconds later, the *Shark's* momentum carried it past *Queen*. Nigel laughed at the sharpshooter hanging off the side of the helicopter waving his fist. He calculated that it would take at least a minute for the pilot to regroup and get back on course. In fact, it took only fifteen seconds.

Damn, concentrate, Nigel. He floored the throttle and headed full speed toward the island. *All I need to do is shake 'em one more time.*

Unable to bear the roller coaster ride anymore, Henri and Mike came storming up the stairs. "Dammit, Nigel. Stop this boat right n—" the judge managed to yell before the crackle of heavy machine-gun fire forced him to dive to the deck.

"What the fuck was that?" Henri screamed to no one in particular. Mike, crouching low on his hands and knees, scanned the skies and saw the *Shark* circling back for round two.

"It's a helicopter," he said pointing at the faint outline growing larger by the moment. "They're trying to kill us."

"More like trying to kill him," Henri pointed toward Nigel.

"Get back down d'ere," Nigel ordered. This time he was brandishing a 9mm Glock handgun. He didn't have to say it twice, as Mike and Henri scrambled below deck. The *Queen* was less than a hundred yards from the island when the *Shark* came in low. This time, the sharpshooter had ditched his machine gun and was behind the controls of what looked like a rocket launcher. Nigel and the sharpshooter both knew this could be his last shot.

Fuck...it's the net, Nigel thought. At the speed they were going, if the net entangled them, it would cause his boat to flip, likely trapping them as it sank. He tried another zigzag, which slowed him down but once again messed up the sharpshooter's aim.

Knowing time was running out, the pilot got tactical. Banking to the left, he sped up for about a hundred yards then made a wide sweeping arc to the right. That put him back head-on with the path of the *Queen*. For a moment it seemed as if the two craft were playing chicken. The boat was almost at the island and the chopper pilot knew that once there, the boat and its crew would be home free, as they'd likely be sheltered in the myriad cays and interlocking lagoons that were the distinguishing features of most of the islands in this region. Henri and Mike huddled together at the bottom of the stairs. The helicopter was heading straight towards them.

"You wan' play?" Nigel mumbled. "Fuck it...let's play."

As the sharpshooter readied his aim, Nigel floored the throttle and began counting.

"5...4..." he whispered. He knew that if he was off by even a second, they were all dead.

"3...2..." The sharpshooter locked his infrared scope onto the forward motion of the *Queen*. He was hoping to put the net right onto her bow.

"Hold on," Nigel yelled. He didn't wait for the one count but instead took a deep breath and, with all his might, pulled the throttle backwards. The *Queen* screeched like a wounded Tyrannosaurus rex. The force nearly threw her occupants into the ocean. Nigel completely flipped over and came down hard on his right side, opening up a nasty gash along his thigh. At that instant, the *Shark's* cannon roared, sending the gigantic net right into the water less than ten yards in front of the *Queen*. Shaking off the pain, Nigel jumped back to the helm and easily maneuvered the *Queen* through the overhanging trees of the island. In no time flat, the boat disappeared from sight. But the *Shark* was used to capturing its prey. For now, it would wait.

Chapter Twenty-Five

IT WAS NEARLY SIX O'CLOCK when Jean-Paul and the rest of the worn and weary reconnaissance team limped into camp. By the way Sammy was gingerly tiptoeing, one might have thought they'd been walking on hot coals. Even Sahara was complaining of fatigue, despite the fact that she was an avid exerciser who ran three miles a day. Although the sun had begun its slow descent behind the horizon, it was still humid, and the temperature felt like it must have been at least in the mid-eighties.

For most of the other castaways, it had been a day jam-packed with heat and boredom. After trying in vain to get Valerie to skinny-dip, Fame decided to go swimming solo. He thrashed about like a harpooned manatee until he swore that he'd seen a great white shark heading toward him, which sent him thrashing back toward shore. He spent the rest of the day by the campfire *begging,* or better yet, talking to Valerie. Shon and Muhammad were gone most of the day on a private adventure in the woods. They had recently returned to teasing and more than a few winks from Fame. Wolf was snoring underneath a nearby tree. Meanwhile, Rachel spent the day down the beach by herself, sitting and staring out into the ocean.

"Honey, we're home," Jean-Paul sang.

Fame quickly stood and with hands on hips cracked, "Y'all couldn't look worse than if you'd been out pickin' cotton all day."

"Shut up," Sahara snapped before plopping down in the sand. Sammy followed her lead.

"Did y'all find anything?" Valerie asked.

"Nope," Murphy said. "We walked all the way around the island in a complete circle."

"Circles?" Fame sounded dejected. "Damn, we gon' die out here. And here my birthday is next month."

"Quit talking crazy, Fame," Jean-Paul snapped. "Nobody wants to hear that foolishness."

"Well what we gonna do?"

Jean-Paul scratched his curls, which had been getting a little more unruly the past few days. "We'll have to ration our food and water even more. And pray."

"Pray for what?" Wolf asked sarcastically, his slumber interrupted by the group discussion. "They ain't no God."

"Uh-oh, you going to hell," Fame joked.

"You should watch your mouth," Shon gasped. "Or else God will really show you suffering."

"Whatever," Wolf smirked. "If you believe that, y'all dumber than I thought."

"You're the dumb-ass. You shouldn't play around with God," Sahara added.

Shon shook her head in disgust at Wolf's blasphemy. "I worship a wonderful God. Just 'cause your black heart is filled with evil, don't try and bring us down." She walked briskly to the hut and searched for her Bible.

"I pray to Allah for your soul, brother," Muhammad said loftily.

Wolf jumped to his feet. "Pray for my soul? Get the hell outta here with that *garbage*! Y'all two just came back from fucking out there in those bushes. What does the Koran say about premarital sex? And you stand here trying to judge me. That's what I hate about all you phony-ass Christians," he paused then looked at Muhammad up and down. "*And* Black Muslims. False-assed prophets feeding folks all that bean-pie-in-the-sky bullshit while they got designer bow-ties and Benzes."

Fame was itching to put in his two cents. "The boy got a point."

If looks could kill, then the glare some of the castaways gave Fame was mass-murderish.

"What y'all looking at?" Fame protested, throwing his hands up. "The preacher at the church I attend has a damn Bentley *and* a bodyguard. What does a man of God need a Bentley for? Why can't he drive a Buick? I thought Jesus rode a donkey!"

"Word," Wolf agreed.

"Y'all are out of your damn minds," Jean-Paul said. "No God? Y'all going to hell."

"Uh-huh," Valerie mumbled.

"Hell?" Wolf asked. "Nigga, I grew up in hell. What kind of God would allow black people to live in them nasty-ass projects? What kind of God would allow innocent women and children to be beaten and abused? Look at all the drugs in the black community!"

"Drugs!?" Sahara said. "How can you talk about drugs when you're a damn drug dealer?"

Wolf got defensive. "I am a victim of my environment."

There was a collective groan of "Oh God."

"What about slavery?" Wolf added. "What kind of God would allow that to happen to a people?"

"What about the Holocaust?" Sammy asked.

"What?" Wolf growled.

Muhammad raised his hand. "I'm sick of people always talking about the damn Holocaust. The Jews lost what, 5 or 6 million people? 100 million Africans died in the slave trade."

"And the Jews get reparations," Wolf added. "We don't."

Fame grinned. "That's because we'd just go out and buy Cadillacs."

"Look," Shon said, returning with her Bible. "I don't profess to know everything about what's in this book, and I'm certainly not an angel."

"You got that right," Fame cracked.

Shon cut her eyes at him. "But I do know that we have no idea what's in God's mind. Everything is not for man to understand."

Muhammad nodded and put his arm around her.

"Cop-out," Fame said. "It says in the Bible to love your fellow man and it's a sin to kill and blah, blah, blah. But then God wipes out whole races of people. Then allows other races to be enslaved and cooked in ovens."

Wolf cut him off. "Plus, we are born to die. And nine out of ten times it's a fucked-up death. Cancer, heart attacks."

"The NYPD," Fame joked.

"Word, the NYPD," Wolf chuckled. "If God loves man so much why does he allow this to happen?"

"Hold up," Sahara said, raising her hand. "Who says God is a he?"

Fame gave her a pitiful look. "If God was a woman, how come men run the world?"

Valerie stood up. "Maybe *she* wants to see how bad y'all fuck it up so that next time we can show you how to do it right."

"You tell 'em, girl," the ladies chimed in, as Valerie gave them all high fives.

Muhammad ignored them. To him the very thought of a female God was blasphemous. "Bottom line is this—Allah has infinite wisdom and man's knowledge is *very* limited."

Jean-Paul nodded his head in agreement. "I read this great book by this guy Lee Strobel. It's called *The Case for Faith*."

"I read that too," Shon said. "Good book."

"I thought the *Bible* was the good book?" Fame asked.

Shon rolled her eyes. "Boy, don't you ever shut up?"

Jean-Paul continued. "In it he said, 'How can a mere finite human being be sure that infinite wisdom would not tolerate certain short-range evils in order for more long-range good that we couldn't foresee?'"

"Can you repeat that in English?" Fame asked.

"Look," Jean-Paul continued. "What is the worst thing that ever happened in the history of the world?"

"That somebody gave *that* motherfucker a boat license," Fame laughed, pointing at Murphy. The castaways doubled over laughing.

"Seriously," Jean-Paul said. What's the worst thing?"

Sammy said, "The Holocaust."

Wolf groaned. "Bullshit. Slavery was the worst thing."

"Me too," Fame agreed.

"I think it was racism," Sahara said.

"What abou—" Jean-Paul began.

"Just say it, nigga," Fame cut him off. "What is the worst thing?"

"Okay, okay. The worst thing to ever happen to the world was the death of Jesus Christ."

"Amen," Shon shouted.

Valerie echoed her sentiment.

Jean-Paul looked around. There wasn't any disagreement other than a frown from Wolf.

"Okay. Now, what was the best thing to ever happen to the world?"

"What is this, *Jeopardy?*" Wolf asked.

Jean-Paul ignored him. "I'll tell you. It was the death of Jesus Christ."

"C'mon," Fame said. "How can it be the *best* and the *worst* thing? That's like finally getting to have sex with Halle Berry, then finding out she had VD."

"You are definitely going to hell," Valerie laughed.

Jean-Paul ignored Fame. "Because Jesus's death meant that *we* can have everlasting life." He paused to let the logic of the statement sink in.

"You can't argue with the truth," Shon said.

"Makes sense—*if* you believe in God," Captain Murphy said.

All eyes turned to the captain. He had been silent during the whole exchange.

"You don't believe in God?" Jean-Paul asked.

"I'm agnostic."

Fame arched his right eyebrow. "You don't believe in God?"

"I said agnostic, not atheist."

"Oh that's that devil worshiper shit, huh?"

The captain was unfazed. "Fame, in a battle of wits you would be considered grossly unarmed."

For once, the comedian stood silent, a confused look all over his face.

"Anyway, an agnostic believes that man doesn't have the capacity to *know* there is a God."

"Man is too stupid?" Jean-Paul asked.

Murphy shook his head no. "Not stupid. It's just impossible for us to know."

"The white man has never known God," Muhammad said, sucking his teeth.

"What's that supposed to mean?" Murphy wanted to know. He seemed hurt by the comments.

Muhammad was matter of fact. "The white man has been the ultimate false prophet. Throughout history he has always come into countries of color and offered the Bible, then followed it up with bullets. He has never known God."

"And I guess a religion that glorifies violence does?"

The eyes of the castaways darted back and forth like spectators at the U.S. Open.

"Ain't that the pot calling the kettle black? Islam is a religion of peace," Muhammad said testily.

"Your prophet Muhammad was one of the most violent Islamic leaders of history. Not to mention Osama bin Laden."

Muhammad waved him off. "What about your great Christian leaders? Charlemagne? Oliver Cromwell? The pope? Man, c'mon. All of the Muslim, African, or Moorish conquerors together can't hold a candle to the death and destruction the white man has committed, usually in the name of Christianity."

"Yeah, and what about the Indians?" Wolf asked. "The Pilgrims came here and fucked them up."

"And on Thanksgiving, too." Fame added. "That's cold-blooded."

Murphy was clearly outnumbered and could only offer a weak protest. "Well, I didn't do it."

"Look," Shon jumped in. "I don't know what this has to do with God, but if you don't believe in God, you're going to hell."

"What *is* hell?" Murphy asked.

Shon closed her eyes and nodded, and said, "Trust me, brother, you'll know it when you get there." A round of amens came from a few of the castaways.

"I don't believe in that fire-and-brimstone version of hell," Jean-Paul said.

"Then you don't believe in hell," Muhammad said.

"You got that right," Shon added.

"What do you mean?" Sahara asked.

He cleared his throat. "I believe that hell is the total absence of God from your life."

"I don't get it," Fame said.

"Well, just imagine the feeling that you get when someone you love with all of your body and soul breaks your heart. I mean stomps on it. You know that empty, barren, dull, throbbing pain that you feel deep down in your heart and stomach? You know, it feels like your very soul is hurting." Jean-Paul paused to let the imagery sink in. "Now magnify that times a billion and that's how you would feel if God left you. That's an unimaginable pain, way more than fire."

"I'd rather deal with that than having my balls on fire," Fame joked.

"Oh, I'm sure it wouldn't be the first time," Sahara cracked.

"Good one," Fame said. "When are you going on tour?"

"Jean-Paul, that's an interesting concept," Sammy said.

Shon clutched her Bible tight. "I don't want to hear it. Hell is the lake of fire."

"Well, one thing's for certain about hell," Wolf said, his lips forming in his devilish grin.

"What's that?" Shon asked.

Wolf bent down and lit a blunt from the campfire. He took a long drag and exhaled. The glow of the campfire made him look extra sinister. "If we don't get off this island soon, we're going to find out if there is one."

Chapter Twenty-Six

A HALF AN HOUR LATER, Nigel slowly and expertly guided *Queen* into a quiet lagoon. Sunlight shimmered off the clear blue waters. The idyllic lagoon was near the opening of a large cave that from outside looked like perfect hideaway. It had taken them no time at all to navigate the twists and turns of the waterway flowing through the island. Mike and Henri thought Nigel seemed to know where he was going. He did. The cave was a rendezvous point he'd used a hundred times before. As Nigel dropped anchor, the judge couldn't hold his tongue any longer.

"Do you mind telling me what in the hell is wrong with you?" Henri yelled at Nigel. His voiced echoed through the deserted lagoon. Nigel was stone-faced, his eyes staring sharp daggers at the judge. His pistol remained tucked in his waistband, but his hand rested gently on the grip. The judge was unfazed by this display of machismo. The situation was so dicey that Mike had to step in between the two men. Henri was so mad his eyes bulged out of their sockets and the danger-ously thick vein snaking down his forehead throbbed. It looked like the San Andreas Fault line. Nigel glowered back, quiet and calm as a cat burglar.

"Well?" Henri demanded, spittle flying from his mouth.

Mike turned and faced Nigel. "What are you? A fugitive?"

The boat captain just shrugged.

"Probably a goddamn drug smuggler," Henri spat. The words tasted like cough syrup. "I know the look. I've sent hundreds like him to prison. Wait until we get back to the main island. I will have you arrested."

Angered at the threat, Nigel yanked a knife from a sheath hidden in the small of his back. "Not if I cut your tongue out first."

Henri flinched and slowly backed away. "What happened to your accent?"

Nigel inched closer. "Shut up. You ask too many damn questions. You better watch what you say, old man. No one has ever snitched on me and lived."

Mike raised his hands in mock surrender. "Calm down, Nigel. People know we are with you. And *nobody* is snitching on *nobody.*" He turned and faced Henri, his eyes pleading with the judge. "Right, Mr. Baptiste?"

Disgusted, Henri turned and walked back down into the cabin. He could be heard mumbling something to the effect of, "Phony-ass accent."

"Nigel, I beg you. He won't say a thing," Mike assured him, a nervous smile on his face. "He's just upset about his son."

"For both of your sakes, he better not say a thing. I won't hesitate to kill both of you."

Mike's nervous smile turned to one of fear. "Nigel, I swear to you, we just want to find Jean-Paul. I don't give a damn what you do for a living. Please don't kill us."

It was Nigel's turn to smile. It was a cruel smile.

"Don't worry. I don't want to kill you either. It's imperative that I find Jean-Paul too."

Mike's right eyebrow nervously arched upward. "Really? Why?"

Nigel sheathed the knife then picked up the red ice chest. "Because he has some very important information that I need."

Nigel then leaped off the boat and walked off in the direction of the cave opening.

Chapter Twenty-Seven

A MAJOR HURRICANE is the most destructive weather force on the planet, capable of wiping out entire cities. The National Hurricane Center classifies their intensity on a scale of one through five. The weakest, a Category 1, has winds ranging from 75 to 95 miles per hour, while a Category 5, the most dangerous, packs winds of 155 plus per hour.

Jeff Berardelli sat back in his chair, popped his second Vivarin of the day, and rubbed the sleep from his eyes. He'd been up for nearly twenty hours tracking the storm. Jeff was a rising star at the Hurricane Center, and he lived for storms. The bigger they were, the better. Surrounded by the center's state-of-the-art computers with their colorful maps and blinking lights, squawking radios, and almost musically screeching printers, Jeff looked like a ship's captain on the command bridge of his vessel.

Jeff was all too aware of how powerful a big storm could be. He had been a forecaster working for WWL, a television station in New Orleans, when Hurricane Katrina destroyed the city in 2005. That storm, only a Category 4, had smashed tens of thousands of homes and ripped open levees like envelopes. When Katrina left town, she also left ninety percent of The Big Easy under twenty feet of water. Katrina destroyed towns along the hundreds of miles of beautiful Mississippi and Alabama coastline. Thousands of people were killed and many more left homeless in her wake. Although Henry was still only a weak Category 2, Jeff knew that with the warm water of the

Caribbean to give it energy, Henry was getting bigger and badder by the hour. Jeff had already alerted all of the remote radar stations throughout the Caribbean and the Gulf and East coasts of the United States. However, it was still too early to give an accurate forecast of the storm's track. All Jeff could do now was wait. He carefully checked and double-checked the radar. The computer models repeatedly came back with the same information. Henry was heading straight for the Bahamas.

Chapter Twenty-Eight

WHILE NIGEL DISAPPEARED INSIDE THE CAVE, Mike went downstairs into the cabin. He placed a sympathetic hand on Henri's hunched shoulders. The judge looked up, a worried expression on his face.

"What have we gotten ourselves into, Michael?"

Mike nervously chewed on his bottom lip while keeping an eye on the cave's entrance. "Don't worry, sir, as long as we cooperate, we'll be fine."

The judge gave him a look he normally reserved for shoplifters. "Cooperate with a smuggler?" He put his face in his hands. "Why, that would be *criminal*."

"We don't have a choice, sir," Mike sighed, sitting down beside him. "Our goal is to find Jean-Paul. Nigel's our only shot."

"Maybe we can overpower him," Henri suggested.

Mike shook his head no. "Sir, we have no idea where we are. We have to trust him. Who gives a shit what he does for a living?"

Resigned to their fate, Henri nodded his head in agreement.

It was then that Nigel exited the cave, wiping sand from his hands.

"He must have buried his contraband," Henri muttered.

Moments later, Nigel effortlessly hopped back into the boat, fished out a Red Stripe, and cracked it open. He took a long swig, his eyes never leaving the two men. They were silent as he quenched his thirst.

Mike broke the silence. "Nigel, you have nothing to worry about from us. We only want to find Jean-Paul."

The boat captain smiled. It was a smile only a mother hyena could love.

Henri cleared his throat. "But before we leave, I have a question."

Nigel nodded. Mike shot Henri a cautious glance.

Undeterred, the judge continued. "Just who are you?"

Nigel's smile turned to a scowl as he pondered the question.

Mike held his breath and looked away at the water.

"I am a smuggler," Nigel finally said.

The judge sneered. "Drugs?"

"Drugs, guns, people. Whatever the market dictates," Nigel added.

"You said Jean-Paul might have some info for you?" Mike asked, emboldened by Nigel's frankness.

Henri's eyes flashed wide. "What kind of information would Jean-Paul have for you?"

"I was scheduled to meet with a very important business associate. His name is Wolf Bailey. He was a passenger on *The King's Dream*. If he is dead, then a lot of people will be out of a lot of money. It is imperative that I know of his whereabouts."

"So that's why you took the job when no one else would?" Henri asked.

Nigel sat down in the captain's chair and cranked up *Queen*. "Look, I figured that we'd either find the survivors or find out if there were no survivors. Either way, I find out what happened to Wolf." He smiled his hyena smile again. "*And* I'd get paid to bring you along."

Mike and Henri stood silently.

"Any more questions?" Nigel asked.

The men shook their heads no.

"Okay, well, let's get back to the search."

It took only minutes for him to guide the boat out a back way. As they exited the interior of the island there was a welcome party waiting just off shore. It was the *Shark*.

Chapter Twenty-Nine

DAY FOUR BEGAN just as the preceding three had, except for one thing: a new level of tension. After a night of fitful sleep, the castaways awakened just after sunrise. They were all in foul moods. By eight o'clock the temperature was hot and humid as ever, and the attitudes were off the charts. Sleeping on sand and piled leaves and twigs can try the best of men or women. Even the calm-tempered Sahara's nerves were coiled tighter than a cobra. She had awakened the castaways at least twice during the night, and everyone was forced to listen to her cursing out Fame, first for his foul-smelling feet and then for his repeated late-night farts. The second time, Fame was so pissed at her that he called a tribal council.

"I'm sick of your bitching," he yelled. "I vote we kick you off of this island."

Sahara was up in a flash standing over him. "Who you calling a bitch, bitch?"

"Both of y'all bitches need to shut the fuck up," Wolf growled.

A silent yet frustrated Jean-Paul got up and walked out of the hut. He figured it was quieter outside.

"Jeeeesus," Fame pleaded to the rest of the half-asleep castaways. "Either she sleeps outside or I will." The vote was unanimous. Fame spent the rest of the night outside.

That morning, the early warnings signs of panic and depression were starting to show on all of their faces. To relieve some of their tension, Jean-Paul, Sahara, and Muhammad went jogging along the beach. Wolf and Fame swam for a while and then smoked up some more of Wolf's stash, which was running dangerously low. Shon read her Bible and walked along the shore. Valerie and Rachel spent most of the morning in hushed conversation. Wolf kept a sharp eye on them from the beach, noticing how animated Valerie seemed to be. Sammy had awakened early and went exploring down the beach. Captain Murphy, sullen and introspective, stared at the horizon for most of the morning as he pondered their worsening situation. He felt that he had to do something, but he was powerless. He knew it was only a matter of time before things on the island would really get dire. The two previous scouting missions had come up empty, and no one was eager to trek into the interior. Without a machete, they had no hope of cutting into the thick interior forest. Besides, who knew what lurked in that green darkness? Poisonous snakes? Wild animals? Food-wise, they were down to two cases of MREs and a handful of PowerBars. Water was a concern too. They had just enough to last them for a week and a half. Tops.

Later, as the day wore on, the castaways slowly drifted back to the camp to escape the brutal heat. While Sahara, Jean-Paul, Captain Murphy, Shon, Muhammad, and Sammy sat around lost in their own thoughts, Fame lay snoring in the shade of the thick Caribbean pines. Every so often he awoke just enough to swat off an ant or a fly. Valerie and Rachel were nowhere to be found. Every now and then one of the members of the group would glance at the shirtless Wolf, who was acting odd. He kept circling the hut, stopping to scan the bushes. Every so often, he'd stare at one of them. *He must be high,* Sahara thought.

"You lose something?" Jean-Paul asked.

Wolf ignored him and stalked back into the hut. The sounds of their mats being tossed and kicked could be heard outside. One by one the castaways got up to see what was going on. Wolf was turning the place upside down.

"Yo, what's wrong with you?" Sahara asked.

"Keep your hands off of my stuff," Shon demanded.

"Fuck me!" Wolf snorted, as he kicked a huge hole in the flimsy wall. A cloud of dust and dirt mixed with straw exploded all over the hut. After the dust settled, Wolf slowly turned and faced the castaways. He was silent as he searched their faces. Wolf had murder in his eyes.

"Where the fuck is my gun?" he demanded.

Chapter Thirty

"TURN OFF YOUR ENGINES!" came the booming voice from the deck of the Coast Guard speedboat. "Put your hands up, we are coming aboard."

"Damn," Nigel sighed, raising his hands. Henri and Mike followed suit.

Holding the bullhorn was Lt. Jack Joseph, and he was pissed. He radioed *Shark,* which was hovering above, and ordered it to maintain its position, guns aimed squarely at *Queen.* Lt. Joseph, a seven-year veteran of the Coast Guard, had chased hundreds of boats and very few had gotten away. His crew had circled the small chain of islands waiting for Nigel to make a getaway. He boarded *Queen,* followed by a chief petty officer, a drug-sniffing German shepherd, and two 9mm-toting seamen.

"Me have a gun, suh" Nigel admitted. "Small of me back. A knife too."

The seamen's trigger fingers tensed. Nigel's fake accent caused Mike and Henri to shoot quick glances at each other.

Lt. Joseph quickly disarmed Nigel. "You have a permit for this?"

"Tis' in me wallet, mon," Nigel said. "Me back pah-ket."

Lt. Joseph fished Nigel's wallet out and rummaged through the contents for the permit. Meanwhile, the chief petty officer led the German shepherd on a search for drugs.

Lt. Joseph turned to Mike and Henri. "Are either of you armed?"

They shook their heads no.

"Why did you flee us earlier?" His voice was hard and stern.

Nigel cleared his throat. "Me don' know who you were. I swear. Fe' t'ought you were a smuggler or somet'ing."

"Bullshit," Lt. Joseph said flatly, eyeing the gun permit. It was legitimate. "What are you doing out here?"

"Searching for dis mon's son," he pointed to Henri. "Da boat he was on, *De King's Dream,* sank a week ago. He come from de states and hire me."

"*King's Dream*?" The lieutenant asked, rubbing his chin in thought. Although he hadn't taken part in the search, he did know of the incident. "Can I see some ID, sir?" Henri handed over his wallet.

"You're a judge?"

"Yes," Henri answered. "Court of Appeals, Fourth Circuit, New Orleans."

Now Lt. Joseph was really confused. "You say your son was on *The King's Dream*?"

"His name is Jean-Paul Baptiste and I came down here to find him."

They were interrupted by the chief petty officer. "The dog found nothing, sir."

Lt. Joseph nodded, then turned back to Henri. "Sir, you are aware that the Coast Guard conducted a thorough search for survivors and found none?"

"But they found no bodies, either," Henri added.

"What about the lifeboat, sir?" the petty officer said.

Mike and Henri's eyes flashed. "What lifeboat?"

Lt. Joseph shot a wicked look at the petty officer.

"Sorry, sir," he sad sheepishly.

"There was a report of a lifeboat spotted floating in these waters that bore the registration of *The King's Dream,* but it was empty."

"Where was it found?" Mike asked. A feeling of hope filled the men.

"About fifteen miles due west of here."

They looked at Nigel. "Me can getcha dere."

They then looked expectantly at Lt. Joseph.

"Well, your paperwork is in order so I'll let you off with a warning. Run away again and you won't get a second chance."

Chapter Thirty-One

"**U**H-OH. Somebody about to get an ass-whipping," Fame cracked over his shoulder while running to hide behind a nearby tree. The castaways stared at Wolf with shocked faces. Their eyes darted back and forth between each other.

Who had the gun?

They looked at each other for any sign of who might have it. All had the same look of relief mixed with disbelief registered on their faces. This was Wolf's nightmare scenario. He no longer had his equalizer, and he was beside himself with anger.

"Where is my fucking gun?" he yelled, kicking up clumps of sand. "I hid it behind the hut before I went swimming." He walked over toward Fame. His gaze was demonic. "Did you take my damn gun? Don't play with me!"

Fame pivoted, trying to keep his tree between him and Wolf. "Wolf, I could think of a hundred niggas I would rather play with before I would even think of playing with you."

Wolf sucked his teeth and turned toward Jean-Paul. "You probably took it, soldier boy," he spat in a low voice. "But I'll still kick your ass, gun or no gun."

"Fuck your gun. And fuck you," Jean-Paul deadpanned.

"Y'all need to calm down," Muhammad cautioned, stepping in between them.

"Jump back, Malcolm X," Wolf snapped.

Muhammad gave him the finger.

"Maybe you just misplaced it," Shon offered.

"I'm glad you lost it," Sahara said, stepping to within a few feet of Wolf. "I know I'm speaking for everyone here. That gun was nothing but trouble."

"I agree," Sammy added.

Wolf raised his hands as if he was a great actor addressing an audience. "I see many of you have all kinds of confidence now, huh? Folks, I don't need a gun to be a gangster."

By this time Rachel and Valerie had walked up. "What's all the commotion about?" Valerie asked.

"He lost his gun," Murphy explained.

"He lost his what?" Valerie gasped.

Wolf stared at Rachel. She was silent and just stood there with a slight grin on her face.

You probably took my fucking gun, he thought. He was in store for some sleepless nights.

"Man, how did you lose the damn gun?" Fame interrupted. "How we gon' hunt?"

Everyone started talking at the same time. Wolf listened to all the individual theories for about thirty seconds before erupting. "All y'all need to shut the fuck up before I start kicking some a—"

In a flash, Jean-Paul was all over Wolf like a swarm of very pissed-off killer bees. It was a moment he'd been waiting for since they'd escaped on the lifeboat. He was raining down blows that were too fast for Wolf to fend off.

"No gun now, huh nigga?" Jean-Paul taunted him. "You ain't so tough now."

Jean-Paul beat Wolf like he had walked in on him in bed with his wife. In a matter of seconds Wolf's head was as lumpy as an old pillow.

"Kick his ass, Jean-Paul," Sammy cheered.

"Damn, he got enough *knots* on his head to get a Boy Scout merit badge," Fame joked. Jean-Paul pushed Wolf to the ground and began kicking him in the side, while Wolf made a noise like air being let out of a tire.

One by one the castaways formed a loose circle around the two combatants. Suddenly, Wolf grabbed Jean-Paul's leg and twisted him to the ground and began pummeling him in the back with both fists.

"Ugh!" Jean-Paul moaned, falling face first in the sand. But he swiftly rolled over and clamped his hands around Wolf's throat and squeezed his neck like an orange.

"Ahh!" Wolf groaned before biting Jean-Paul's hand. Wincing with pain, he released his death grip immediately. For the next few minutes, the two men thrashed around in the sand like roosters at a cockfight. The crowd was definitely not on Wolf's side.

"Get 'em, JP," Muhammad urged.

"Bust his black ass," Valerie yelled, throwing a stick that hit Wolf in the back.

The two men were on their feet now, gasping for air. They both looked as if they had spent the night locked in a closet with Mike Tyson. Jean-Paul's left eye had a big black ring around it. Wolf, with his right jaw swollen, lip bloodied, and slobber running out of the corner of his mouth, managed to dodge a thunderous left hook before clutching Jean-Paul in a bear hug. With his arms pinned to his side, Jean-Paul was defenseless. Wolf slammed Jean-Paul down hard. His right side crunched to the ground like a sack of potato chips. The thud was sickening. The women gasped. For a moment Jean-Paul lay motionless.

"Aw shit," Fame blurted. "He dead."

Sahara smacked him upside the head. "Shut up."

"Get up Jean-Paul," the castaways cheered.

He wasn't dead, just dazed, and coughing up a mouthful of sand. Jean-Paul slowly struggled to one knee. His shook his head from side to side. Meanwhile, Wolf crawled over to a nearby pile of rocks and picked one up. His intent was clear. As he turned, Jean-Paul threw a handful of sand right into his eyes.

"Fuck!" Wolf yelled.

Temporarily blinded, he dropped the big rock and flailed his arms is the air. As the cobwebs cleared from his head, Jean-Paul ran toward Wolf as fast he could before launching himself into an awkward flying drop-kick. His foot caught Wolf squarely in the stomach. As Wolf doubled over, Jean-Paul, heaving and sucking in gulps of air, looked at the castaways. His next move was decided for him. They gave a thumbs-down that would have made a mob of ancient Romans proud. Jean-Paul then let loose an uppercut that came from way down in Mississippi. When his fist connected with Wolf's face, it sounded like a firecracker. Seconds later, Wolf lay crumpled on the ground like Rodney King.

Chapter Thirty-Two

WHILE SAHARA RUSHED INSIDE THE HUT to grab the first-aid kit, a few of the castaways gently eased Jean-Paul down against a nearby boulder. Out of breath and with his face covered in dirt and sweat, he looked like a homeless person. As he sipped some water, Sahara rubbed alcohol on his various cuts and scratches. He flinched as the liquid stung his skin.

"Aw, did I hurt the baby?" Sahara teased.

Jean-Paul winced but remained silent. So she slathered on some more.

"Ouch!" he yelped.

"Don't worry, you'll get a lollipop when I'm done," she said.

He grinned. "I better get something."

He got more alcohol.

"Ow, okay, okay," he joked. "What are my chances for survival?"

"Better than his," she pointed at Wolf, who was sprawled out on the ground, out cold, snoring. He looked like a big black Doberman.

"Speaking of, what are we going to do with him?" Muhammad asked.

"We should tie him up," Fame said.

They all looked at him as if he was crazy.

"What?" the comedian said defensively. "You know when he wakes up it's gon' be on again."

Sammy nodded. "He's right. He was going to kill you, man."

"He wasn't going to do anything," Jean-Paul countered.

"My ass," Fame said. "He was 'bout to crack your damn skull with that big-ass rock."

"I'm with Fame on this one," Muhammad said. "Let's tie him up." He then went off looking for some vines to use as rope.

"I agree," Shon echoed.

Jean-Paul shook his head no.

Captain Murphy sighed and rubbed the back of his neck. "Maybe we should force him out of the group somehow."

Sahara was unconvinced. "Where would he go? How would he survive?"

"Who cares?" Sammy asked.

"We have to watch our backs," Shon said.

Fame sucked his teeth. "We already have to watch our backs around his ass."

All of a sudden Wolf started coughing. The castaways froze, each one holding their breath. Then just as quickly, he passed out again.

Rachel finally spoke up. "Why don't we kill him?"

It got real quiet. Then the castaways exploded with laughter.

"Girl, you're crazy," Sahara laughed.

"I'm no murderer," Sammy said.

"Kill him? We gon' call you the Black Widow," Fame snorted.

Jean-Paul stood up and raised his arms. "We're forgetting the most important thing."

"What?" they asked.

"The gun," he said. "Now who here has it?"

Silence.

"C'mon now. Who has it? This is important. Our lives depend on it."

They stared at each other, but no one was giving up the goods.

Sammy offered, "Maybe he lost it."

Sahara shook her head. "I don't think so."

Jean-Paul was adamant. "Someone here has it."

The castaways continued to stare at each other.

"But until someone admits to it," Muhammad said, "I'm getting something to tie his ass up with."

Chapter Thirty-Three

A COOL BLANKET OF NIGHT descended on the castaways, but it competed with the warm glow of the roaring campfire, which sent sparks high into the night sky. It was the best the wood had burned since they hit the island, and this night, it also seemed as if every little star in the heavens had an extra bit of twinkle. If any of the castaways had been astronomers, they would have noticed a very distinctive constellation overhead, Orion—a constellation that could have been interpreted as an omen. In Greek mythology, Orion was a great hunter who boasted that he was a match for any animal on earth. The goddess of the hunt, Artemis, cared for him so much that she placed him among the stars after he died. And to prevent him from being alone in the sky, the Dog (Canis Major) was later added to assist Orion in his hunting. It's an old story. The hunted sometimes bags the hunter.

"Ouch, where the hell am I?" Wolf moaned. He was still seeing double, triple even. He raised his hands in an attempt to massage his throbbing temples. He couldn't. His hands were tied behind his back.

"What the f—?" He squirmed, trying to make sense of his situation.

Wolf's swollen head felt like a badly used piñata. He had the kind of headache that couldn't be eased with anything less than morphine or a guillotine. Wolf tried in vain to blink the foggy vision from his eyes. The darkness of night combined with the brightness of the campfire didn't help his focus. As his vision slowly cleared, he figured he must be dreaming when he saw the shadowy forms of the castaways standing around the blazing campfire. They looked like a Sioux war party. Or Zulus. Or vigilantes. Each wore a grim face, and each held some type of primitive weapon. Jean-Paul and Murphy sported sharp bamboo sticks. Sahara and Muhammad gripped makeshift clubs. They looked like cavemen. The rest of them held rocks of various sizes and sharpness. Fame held a bag of pork and beans. He was too hungry for revolution.

"I'm nonviolent," the comedian had claimed. "Besides, y'all don't look like the Crips or the Bloods, but more like the crippled and the bloody."

I must be high, Wolf thought as he took in the motley crew.

"He's awake," he heard Jean-Paul tell the others. Clearly, he had emerged as the de facto leader. "No, you're not dreaming, Wolf. We are tired of your shit and we wanted to let you know that you will not be tolerated anymore. We've got your gun and your knife."

Wolf gave him a cold hard stare.

Sahara interrupted, "And we will beat the black off of your ass if you step out of line." She waved a thick club made from a tree branch for emphasis.

Wolf smirked. "All of you feel that way?"

They remained silent but the way they held their weapons spoke volumes. Jean-Paul walked to within inches of Wolf. "Don't be fooled Wolf, we are serious. I will kill you if I have to."

Jean-Paul stood, made a sweeping gesture with his hands toward the castaways. "We had a vote. Some wanted to tie you up and keep you tied up until we left the island." Jean-Paul shook his head from side to side. "Too impractical." He looked at Rachel. "Others wanted to *kill* you outright. Leave your body for the warthogs to chew on. But we think the best course of action is to kick your ass out."

Wolf's eyes widened. "Kick me out. Motherfucker, where are you kicking me *out* to? What the hell is this?"

Muhammad stepped to the forefront. "The other side of the island."

"And how am I supposed to survive?" Wolf grimaced, his wrists burning from the tight vines.

Jean-Paul sucked his teeth. "We'll give you a few MREs and a little bit of water, but once that's gone, you're on your own."

"Aw c'mon," Wolf protested. "I'll die out there. We have to stick together."

Sahara, angered by his hypocrisy, said, "Stick together? You didn't think about that when you were flashing that cannon, trying to act all bad."

"What did you say to me? You don't do that brotherhood shit," Muhammad reminded him.

"What do I have to do to make up it to you guys?" Wolf pleaded.

The castaways rolled their eyes.

A desperate Wolf continued to squirm in his binds. "I mean it. Look at me. What am I going to do?"

"I tell you what, Wolf," Jean-Paul grinned. "We'll sleep on it."

Wolf was silent for a few seconds. "Okay, that's fair," he admitted before partially turning his body over to reveal his binds to be cut.

The castaways ignored him and turned to go inside the hut.

"Hey, where y'all going? Aren't you going to cut me loose?"

Rachel shook her head no. "Didn't you hear, asshole? We said that we'd sleep on it."

The castaways laughed.

"Girl, you got spunk," Fame joked. "I'ma call you Spunky Brewster."

"But I'm hungry," Wolf pleaded.

"Eat a dick," Valerie offered.

Rachel was the last one into the hut but before walking through the door, she turned and looked at Wolf. She had pure, uncut hate in her eyes. He stared back defiantly. She slowly mouthed the words, "I... am... going... to... kill...*you*."

All Wolf could do was squirm and smile. But it was a very nervous smile.

Chapter Thirty-Four

T HE CASTAWAYS HAD FILED ONE BY ONE inside their hut, and although it was dark none of them were sleepy. Still keyed up from their altercation with Wolf, many of them made small talk as they sat or lay down on their makeshift beds of straw and leaves. It was dark except for the stars and light from the campfire. The castaways weren't going to sleep anytime soon. Not with a hungry and wounded Wolf just outside their door.

"Are we really going to leave him out there all night?" Shon asked.

The high-pitched voice of Fame screeched from the back of the hut. "Do you want him to sleep next to you?"

"Why don't you shut up?" Sammy snapped.

Fame was mildly outraged. "I *know* the Cream of Wheat Man ain't trying to act all tough?"

"Real tough now, huh, Fame?" Sahara asked. "You weren't so tough out there with Wolf."

Valerie shook her head. "Un-uh. Punk-ass was eating pork and beans."

"Well," Fame shot back, "there is a big difference between Wolf and the Cream of Wheat Man here."

Sammy had had enough of the slights and jumped to his feet. He blindly stumbled in the dark, searching for Fame.

"Ouch," Shon yelped. "Get off my feet."

"Watch my arm, nigga," Valerie barked.

"Sorry," Sammy apologized. "Fame, where are you?"

By that time Fame had crawled over to the other side of the hut. "Smile Sammy, I'll find *you*," he cracked. A few of the castaways snickered.

"Just wait until tomorrow," Sammy warned. "I'll kick Cream of Wheat out of your ass."

"Hey Sammy." It was Murphy flipping on the flashlight. "Why are you so upset with him calling you the Cream of Wheat Man?"

It was dark, but there was just enough light for Murphy to see Sammy rolling his eyes. "What?" he answered. "It's a black thang."

"Then how would you know?" Valerie joked.

"Good one," Fame added.

"I'm serious," Murphy went on. "Fame called you the Cream of Wheat Man but Valerie called you a nigg—"

Before Murphy could finish, there was a chorus of "What the hell did you say?" or "Hold up a second, white boy."

"Were you about to call him a nigger?" Muhammad asked.

"Uh, hold on," Captain Murphy protested. "I was just, uh..."

"You were 'bout to just get yo' ass kicked," Valerie assured him.

Murphy cleared his throat. "I was using the word *nigg*—"

"Watch it!" Sahara blurted.

"Okay, I was using the N-word in the context of a question."

Sahara stood up. "I don't care what the context was. White people can't use the word *nigger*."

"That's right," Valerie said.

"Why not?" Murphy asked.

Silence. Then came an avalanche of remarks: "Oh goodness," from Fame. "What?" from Valerie. And "Please, just don't go there," from Muhammad.

"I don't understand," Murphy asked. "Why can't we talk about it?"

"It is a black thang, you wouldn't understand," Muhammad said.

"Doesn't matter," Sammy said. "They *can't* explain. They call each other niggers and bitches and whores but they get upset when the white man does it. It's a warped logic that black people have some special right to go ahead and degrade other black people, so long as nobody else does."

Valerie harrumphed, "You shouldn't even open your Uncle-Tom-ass mouth. You with a white woman."

"At least I have someone who loves me," Sammy snapped. "I'm not running around sucking off ballplayers with nothing to show for it."

"Fuck you!" Valerie yelled.

"You don't know anything about us," Rachel added.

Sammy waved her off and turned on his side.

"Touchy subject, eh?" Murphy asked.

"Damn right it's a touchy subject," Muhammad agreed. "Why do you even give a shit what we say to each other? You and your white friends all probably call us niggers when you're not around black people."

"You're right," Murphy agreed.

There was absolute silence. Even the crickets stopped chirping.

"Come again?" Jean-Paul asked.

"I *know* this motherfucker just didn't?" Valerie said.

"Oh yes he did!" Rachel confirmed.

"Time to untie Wolf," Fame warned.

"So what?" Murphy sighed. "I'm Irish and Irishmen don't lie. And I don't give a flying fag's fart about fighting no man, black or white. Yes, my mates and I might say *nigger* every now and then, or *black bastards,* but we don't mean any harm. It's just something to say. We also say *chinks, kikes, guineas, rag-heads* and call ourselves *mick bastards.* But I would never refuse a man in need whether he was black, yellow, or goddamn purple."

Muhammad sat up, shaking his head with an "I told you so" look written all over his face. "That proves it, I knew all of you crackers were the same."

"All white people aren't the same," Sammy interjected.

Valerie was disgusted. "Ugh, he makes me sick."

"And I'm sure you've made more than a few men sick," Sammy snapped back.

"Ooh, he got you," Fame said.

Sahara was still astonished by Captain Murphy's comment. "I can't believe you just admitted that," she said in a pensive voice.

"I'ma pray for you," Shon said.

Murphy cleared his throat, and if the others could've seen his face they would have detected a sly smile. "I'll also tell you this. I think black people are sometimes their own worst enemies."

"You better shut up," Muhammad warned.

"Why?" Sammy said, coming to Murphy's defense. "Let the man speak. The captain has a right to speak."

Fame bugged his eyes dramatically. "Yassa boss, let massa speak on it."

Sammy flipped him the bird.

"I'm liking this," Jean-Paul said, clearly enjoying the debate. "When was the last time you ever heard a white man speaking this freely? Go 'head, Cap'n."

"Some black people, and the emphasis is on *some* black people, they deal and use drugs in their own neighborhoods, they kill each other, they drink themselves to death, they take the street mentality to their jobs, they have no desire for advanced education, and they are lazy and generally have no plan for the future."

"Lazy?" Muhammad asked. "Black people are lazy? Then why were we always the maids, or butlers, valets, nannies, drivers, shoeshine boys, or gardeners? If we're so lazy, why are white people always sitting on their asses relaxing while we do all the damn work?"

"One word," Murphy said. "Education."

Muhammad threw up his hands and moaned, "Aww."

"But it's not all of our faults," Shon jumped in.

"I know," Murphy said. "It's the white man's fault, right?"

"You think you're funny, huh?" Muhammad asked. "Right now I really want to put my foot in your ass. But that might too *black* of me."

"That would be right fine niggardly of you," Fame cracked.

Muhammad ignored him. "The white man likes to fight his battle with words. Here are some words for you. What about how you stole millions of Africans and made them slaves in a foreign land? Erased their languages, cultures, and religions for hundreds of years while denying them any taste of education. Fed them the least nutritious parts of the lowest of animals, in effect altering their physiology to where many of us, their descendants today, are genetically predisposed to diseases we never had in Africa. You used their sweat, tears, blood, and strong backs to build the American Dream, while they were living a nightmare."

"Preach nigga!" Fame shouted.

The other castaways sat spellbound.

Muhammad continued. "Then they unleashed these same illiterate people into a society with no viable means of support, stripped them of any civil rights, and literally re-enslaved them with illegal and immoral laws designed to reduce this race of humans to the status of animals. Gave the world such an exaggerated, sinister, and distorted depiction of us on your minstrel shows, stage plays, and movies that even the lowest untouchable in the poorest street in Calcutta thinks they're better than a dirty old nigger. You want to know why niggers don't give a damn? It's because all of what I just said is encoded in our DNA. The white man raped us, lynched us, and lied to us. So fuck you, Captain Murphy, and fuck all of your redheaded, potato-eating, pint-of-Guinness-stout-drinking Irish mick-bastard friends. Think about *that* the next time you call me a nigger."

"Ooo wee," Valerie cackled, clapping.

Rachel clapped too. "You tell that cracker-ass cracker."

"What you have to say about that, Cap'n?" Shon asked.

"Can I be frank?" Murphy asked.

"And you haven't been already?" Jean-Paul shot back.

"You guys are always talking that black shit," Murphy explained. "Instead of wasting your breath on your protest of the month or reparations that you won't get—or even if you do they're coming right back to the white man—why not try taking some action? I'll let you in on a secret—the so-called white man, the one who is keeping his rich oxfords on your poor black necks? He doesn't give a flying fuck about what you say. He never did and he never will. No matter what you say. Hell, he doesn't give a damn about poor *white* people. Think he cares about you? And the poor white people? They don't give a damn either because they have their own problems. Now the middle-class white people will act like they give a damn, so they can use your talents to make them rich so that they won't have to listen to bullshit from the Reverend Jesse 'Baby Daddy' Jackson or the Reverend Al Sharp-tongue."

"Yo, Al *really* needs to get rid of that perm," Fame cracked.

"You may be the first honest white man in the history of the world," Sammy said, shaking his head and smiling.

Murphy continued. "And for crying out loud, quit thinking you're the only race who has had it bad. The Irish lost people. The Italians lost people. The Jews lost people in the Holo—

Muhammad threw up his hands. *"Allahu Akbar.* Again! I'm so *sick* of people always talking about the damn Jews! They lost what, 6 million people in the Holocaust? *A hundred million Africans* died in the Middle Passage. You *never* hear about that! Why!?"

"Cuz we don't stick together and create and support museums and films to remind people," Jean-Paul said.

"We're just crabs in a barrel," Fame said.

Murphy leaned forward. "I *know* you guys aren't naive enough to think that other races don't call you niggers. Y'all call us *Casper, honkies, white bread,* and a whole host of other things."

"Crackers! You forgot crackers," Fame said.

"I forgot—crackers," Captain Murphy laughed.

"But that's different," Rachel chimed in.

"Why?" Murphy asked.

Rachel shrugged. "It just is."

That wasn't a good enough answer for Murphy. "So, how is it again you can call us names, but we can't call you names?"

Muhammad smiled, at last. "It's a black thing, Murphy. You wouldn't understand."

"Try me," Murphy said dryly, growing testy with Muhammad's bitter rants. "Everything isn't black or white. There's a whole spectrum of gray out there, too."

Muhammad shook his head in disgust. "See, that's what I'm talking about."

Murphy had a confused look on his face.

"Why does it have to be *black*?" Muhammad explained. "Why can't it just be *white*?"

This time the other castaways had confused looks on *their* faces.

"White people throw the word *black* around too casually. For instance, everything that's *black* is bad," Muhammad said.

"You're not making any sense," Murphy said.

Muhammad frowned. "Like *black*-eye, *black*-mark, *black*-magic is bad but *white* magic is good. Why is that?"

"Um-huh," someone murmured.

Murphy sat stonefaced, clearly in the dark about Muhammad's comments.

"I got one," Valerie chimed in. "Why is that the *bad* guy in the movie wears a *black* hat but the *good* guy's hat is white?"

"Yeah," Muhammad said.

Murphy looked away, chewing his bottom lip. For some reason, he was feeling slightly embarrassed and more than a little taken aback. "You guys are conspiracy theorists."

Muhammad sucked his teeth. "Why is that *black* ice is bad, but *white* snow is pure and creates a winter wonderland?"

The group chuckled.

"I got one." It was Sahara and she was smiling. "Why is it that in Rome when they pick a Pope, *black* smoke is bad but *white* smoke is good?"

"What about *black*-out?" Rachel asked.

"Yeah, and *black*-balled," Valerie added.

"*Black*-hole," Jean-Paul laughed.

"*Black*-death," Fame joked. "And *black* cats are bad luck."

What is this, a game? Murphy thought.

"The descendants of Ham are supposed to be *black* and cursed," Shon said.

"But you know black people love some ham," Fame cracked.

"Why is it that when the stock market crashes it's *Black* Monday or some other black day?" Muhammad said, adding fuel to the fire.

"Hey," Fame interrupted. "The day after Thanksgiving is *Black*

Friday. They should call it White Friday because most black people are too broke to go shopping."

Murphy sighed and dropped his face in his hands.

Muhammad stood up and spread his arms, taking all of them in with his gesture. "Why is it that if you're in a bad spot, you're behind the eight-ball—which is black?"

The group laughed and cheered, "Preach on *black*-man."

"Conspiracy against black is everywhere," he continued. "Take a simple game like pool for example. The cue-ball is the most important ball on the table and it's what color?"

"White," someone called out.

"That's right. *White*. The table's surface is green like the Earth and the *white* ball tries to put all of the colored balls in the hole, like the *red* ball."

Fame raised his hand. "The Indian?"

"Correct," Muhammad said. "The *yellow* ball?

"Orientals," Valerie answered.

"Asians," Muhammad clarified. "And who does the *white* ball save for last?"

"The eight-ball," the group said in unison.

Muhammad smiled. "The *black* ball. The black man."

The castaways applauded. Muhammad smiled and bowed slightly.

Murphy shook his head in amazement, wondering how the crew could be so cordial to him individually but gang up on him in a group setting. "Wait a second," he said. "Who came up with the term "black" to talk about black people in the first place? It was black people, back in the Sixties. 'Black power,' 'black pride.' You're not making any sense."

Muhammad smiled bitterly. "And what were they trying to do when they did that? Change they way everybody had always felt about that word, about that *idea—especially black people*. They wanted to try to change how we ourselves had become ashamed of our darkness, our non-whiteness. Our blackness."

"Black is beautiful, baby," Sahara added in a husky tone, raising her eyebrows and smiling at the now-quiet Murphy.

Muhammad took a deep breath and continued. "Look, no other race has been psychologically manipulated like black people. For damn near a millennium it's been drilled into our heads by white people that we're inferior, and I for one truly believe that it has altered the way our brains process information regarding race. Bottom line, we feel that as a people we have been treated the worst, so in our minds there is a double standard when it comes to racial issues."

"So black people get a free pass?" Murphy asked.

"You damn right!" the group shouted.

Fame stood up. "That socio–psycho-political shit is all fine, but you know what's the main difference between white and black folks?"

"What?" Murphy asked, expecting a joke.

"White people let their dogs lick them on the face and mouth."

"Huh?"Murphy said.

"Think about it," Fame continued. "You see white folks in the parks damn near tongue-kissing their dogs. You never see black people doing that. And y'all call us nasty."

"That's true," Valerie said. "I can't stand no dog licking on me."

"There is so much I can say about that," Fame joked, sitting back down.

"Jesus," Sammy muttered under his breath.

"Judas," Fame shot back.

"What is your goddamn problem?" Sammy snapped.

Fame waved him off dismissively. "You're the one with the problem, Uncle Tom."

Sammy bolted upright. He was seething, "You know something, asshole?"

Fame shrugged him off and turned over on his side.

"You call me an Uncle Tom?" Sammy asked, his voice rising. "You're a Sambo."

A ripple of giggles could be heard from the group.

"How you figure that, Clarence Thomas?" Fame shot back.

Sammy knew he'd gotten Fame's goat, and a little smile came to his lips. "Buffoons like you have done *way* more damage to the image of African Americans than so-called Uncle Toms. For hundreds of years, idiots like you have been clowning for white folks, setting the race back in the process. Let me school you on some black comedic history. Ever hear of Billy Kersands?"

Fame's face was blank.

"Figures," Sammy said. "Billy was an early nineteenth-century black comedian who entertained white folks. His big thing? Stuffing two billiard balls in his mouth."

Murphy rubbed his own jaw at the thought.

"Ever hear of Bert Williams?" Sammy added.

Once again there was silence.

"You call yourself a comic? You don't even know your history. Bert Williams was the first black crossover comic. He made a fortune during the late 1800s and early 1900s clowning for white people. The list is endless. Oh, and check out their names. Mantan Moreland. Chuck and Chuckles. Buck and Bubbles. Stepin Fetchit. Let's add Fame to that list. While great men like W.E.B. DuBois were trying to uplift the race, minstrels like you were pulling us down like crabs in a barrel.

"Way I see it, Fame, comedians like you will do whatever for a dollar," Sammy continued. "Look how Hollywood uses comedians to perpetuate stereotypes. They put y'all in dresses, got y'all shucking and jiving, doing everything but chasing chickens and eating watermelon. The only thing missing is the blackface."

The group held their breath, anticpating a witty comeback from Fame. They were disappointed.

"Whatever," Fame weakly retorted. "What about Richard Pryor?"

"Fame, your sorry ass sure ain't no Richard Pryor," Valerie shot back.

Sammy nodded in agreement. "Ain't that the truth. Richard Pryor was a genius. He had his his demons, but he didn't just change black comedy—he changed all of comedy. You shouldn't even try to compare yourself to Chris Rock, let alone Richard Pryor. You're nothing more than the second coming of Stepin Fetchit. Always acting a damn bumblin' clown. I mean, look at you out here. We're fighting to save our lives, and you screw up the simplest of tasks. You're lazy. You're dumb. You're little more than a modern-day minstrel. I might be with a white woman—in fact, I *love* me some of this white woman—but at least I'm a role model for black achievement. It's clown-ass niggers like you who give black people a bad name."

Once again the group looked at Fame, but he just stormed out of the hut.

"Whoa!" Jean-Paul said.

Sahara shook her head in amazement. "That's the first time since we've been on this island that something's made Fame speechless."

Chapter Thirty-Five

THE NEXT MORNING, for the first time since they'd arrived on the island, Fame was the first one awake. A giant horsefly had landed on his face and he wound up slapping himself out of his sleep. Ever since his most recent farting incident the castaways had made him sleep near the entrance, ass out and directed downwind.

It was shortly before dawn and Fame's stomach was growling like a tiger. He knew the policy on rations, but he figured that since everyone was asleep, no one would notice if he helped himself to a piece of MRE marble cake. He eased himself up slowly and tiptoed out of the hut, so as not to wake anyone up. His belly growled again, but what he saw outside of the hut really turned his stomach.

"Oh my God," he yelled, and ran back into the hut. "Wake up! Wake up!"

One by one the castaways were startled awake, wiping the morning cold from their eyes. They all stared at Fame standing in the doorway. His face was ashen. Jean-Paul was on his feet in seconds and reaching for a weapon, a reflex action from his Army days. "What's wrong?"

An ominous feeling came over Murphy and he reached for his stick. "Is it Wolf?"

Fame nodded.

"What is it?"

"He's gone."

"Gone?"

Fame nodded.

"Oh shit," Valerie said, putting her hands to her mouth.

"Where?" Muhammad asked.

"I don't know," Fame shook his head. "He was gone when I came outside. And that's not all."

Jean-Paul's face was stern. "I should have stood watch. Guys, grab your weapons and follow me."

All of the men picked up their rocks or clubs or sticks and followed Jean-Paul out the door. All of them except for Fame

"What are you doing standing there?" Sahara asked.

"He's scared," Valerie said.

Fame was defensive. "No, I'm not."

"Then why aren't you outside with the other *men*?" Rachel inquired.

Fame just stood there chewing his bottom lip.

"What a punk," Sahara said before picking up a rock and running out of the door.

Chapter Thirty-Six

THE SUN SAT HIGH IN THE MIDDAY SKY, the seas were calm, and Nigel's head was tilted back under yet another can of very cold Red Stripe. After draining it, he wiped the streaks of brew from the sides of his mouth and let out a deafening burp.

"Is that a mating call for the humpback whale?" Mike teased. Nigel winked. After a couple of days of being chased by the Coast Guard, Nigel was ready to get back to doing what they'd paid him to do: Find Jean-Paul...and Wolf.

"Where do we start?" The judge asked.

Nigel squinted at the chart. "Here," he said, as he pointed toward a strip of isolated islands. "There are only a few places around here that are close enough to where they were last heard from."

"How far are we from the nearest island?" Mike wanted to know.

"An hour, maybe two."

"What are the odds that we will find anyone, or anything?" Henri sighed, eyeing the horizon.

Mike's eyes lit up. He was surprised at the comment. Clearly, the strain of the whole adventure was wearing on the judge. "What do you mean, odds? You're not losing hope, are you, sir?"

Henri shook his head and kept his gaze on the horizon. "No, I'm just being realistic. It has been more than a week."

Nigel would hear none of it. "We will find your boy. Nothing will stand in my way." The captain paused for a moment before smiling like he was posing for a yearbook picture. "The only thing that can stop us would be a hurricane."

Chapter Thirty-Seven

"HURRICANE HENRY," the announcer said, "is now a Category 3 storm and if it follows its present course, Henry is expected to hammer the Bahamas within the next few days."

The announcer's voice sounded almost apocalyptic. Jeff Berardelli smiled at the taped promo to his appearance on CNN. He always found it amusing the way the news media seem to sensationalize everything. They made disasters sound like sporting events. Jeff, after all, was a meteorologist, and as a scientist he was not prone to fantasy. As a technician carefully clipped on his microphone and an assistant dabbed on the last of his makeup, he was judged ready for prime time. Jeff was being interviewed live via satellite from the National Hurricane Center in Miami.

"Welcome Jeff," said the beautiful brunette anchor. "Can you give us the latest position and track of the storm?"

Jeff turned to face a massive bank of blinking computers and monitors. It looked like the bridge of the starship *Enterprise*. He took out a telestrator and began highlighting the swirling mass that was Henry. "Henry is located roughly 200 miles off the coast of the Grand Bahamas isle."

One of the producers in the control room asked the beautiful anchor to ask Jeff about the winds.

"Jeff, what about the winds?"

"Right now there are sustained winds of 125 miles an hour."

The anchor's eyes widened. "Boy, she's packing quite a punch."

"He," Jeff corrected.

"Excuse me, *he*," she said. "What kind of damage can a Category 3 do?"

"Varies. The biggest problem is the storm surge, which is generally nine to twelve feet above normal. You'll probably have some structural damage to small residences and utility buildings, causing power failure. There will be lots of blown-down trees and shrubbery. Evacuation is possible for low-lying residences along the shore."

"What are the chances that Henry might become a Category 4 or 5?"

Jeff rubbed his baby-faced chin. "Very good, especially with all the warm water it has to fuel it."

The anchor was busy scribbling down information on her pad. "What about damage and devastation?"

"Total," Jeff finished.

Chapter Thirty-Eight

JEAN-PAUL LOOKED AT MURPHY and shook his head in disbelief.

"What do you think?" Captain Murphy asked.

"It's safe to say that he's not there," Jean-Paul said sarcastically.

The men stared at the area where Wolf had been tied up. All that was left were large grooves in the sand.

"Probably from where he twisted out of his binds," Muhammad observed.

There were also scattered strips of dried vines. Jean-Paul bent down and picked one up. Disgusted he quickly threw it back in the sand. "Some handcuffs," he spat. "A three-year-old could have gotten out of these brittle-ass vines."

The men looked at Muhammad, who looked defensive. "I tied them as tight as I could." He pointed at Jean-Paul. "You're the army man. We should have had a guard."

Jean-Paul eyed him back, hard. Muhammad tried to return the glare, but his eye quickly veered to the ground. He had witnessed how ferociously Jean-Paul had fought Wolf and he wasn't eager to be his next bout.

"Now's not the time to blame each other. We've got to find Wolf," Sahara said.

"She's right," Murphy said.

"Where could he have gone?" Sammy asked.

They all looked to the surrounding woods and on the ground. No sign of Wolf. There were so many footprints around the campsite that it was impossible to be certain who had made them.

"He might be out there in the woods looking at us right now," Sahara said ominously.

It was at that moment that the rest of the women came outside— all except for Shon. Valerie and Rachel had worried looks all over their faces.

"Oh my goodness," Valerie said. "Where is he?"

The men shook their heads. Rachel was silent, in a near state of shock. She ran back into the hut. Valerie ran back in behind her.

"What are we going to do?" Sahara asked.

The men turned to Jean-Paul.

"I want to know one thing first," he said. "Does anybody here have Wolf's gun or knife? This is no time to play. All of our lives are on the line now."

It was silent as each of them searched the faces of the other castaways.

"Okay. I know where the knife is," Fame finally admitted, rather sheepishly.

The castaways were stunned. "Huh? Where?" said Sammy.

"I hid it," he said.

Jean-Paul was exasperated. "Hid it where? We need it now."

Fame quickly led them to a small hole that he had dug a few feet from the hut. Twigs and a rock, which he brushed away, disguised it. Fame knelt and dug through the sand to reveal the switchblade. Fully extended, its length was twelve inches. Jean-Paul snatched it from him.

"Why in the hell did you keep this a secret?"

Fame threw up his hands. "Look, I didn't want anybody to get killed around here."

Sahara was unconvinced. "I bet he has the gun, too."

The castaways slowly moved in on the cowering Fame.

The comedian clasped his hands together as in prayer. "I swear on my dead grandmother plus two good white people that I don't have the gun. I'm scared of guns. As a kid I didn't even play with water guns."

"Your dead grandmother? I thought you told me you grew up in an orphanage," Sammy asked.

Fame looked at the ground. "Well, I had to have had a grandmother somewhere."

Jean-Paul unfolded the switchblade and held it right up to Fame's face. The blade glinted in the early morning sunlight. "If you're lying about the gun, I swear I am going to cut your tongue out."

"I swear to God, I don't know where the gun is," Fame pleaded.

Jean-Paul folded the knife back and stuck it in his pocket. With a wave of his hand he gathered everyone around him. "All right guys, here's what we are going to do. Muhammad, I want you to go around and check the area in back of the hut. Sammy, take a look along the beach for any fresh footprints." Jean-Paul was barking orders like a drill sergeant. "Captain Murphy, come with me and we will search the woods. Fame, stay back here and guard the women," he finished, knowing it was more likely that if it came down to it, the women would end up protecting Fame.

"Jean-Paul?" It was Sahara. She had just come from beside the hut with a worried look on her face.

"Yes?" he answered. The other castaways stopped what they were doing to listen.

"Wolf stole our food."

"What?" they all roared. Everyone ran to the side of the hut to see for themselves. They crowded around the supply boxes and groaned. Jean-Paul couldn't see over them.

"Did he take all of it?" Jean-Paul asked.

"No," Sahara answered. "But it looks like he took all he could carry."

Fame put his face in his hands. "We gon' starve to death."

Jean-Paul pushed his way through and inspected the remaining MREs and water bottles. He frowned. "Looks like we only have enough supplies left for a few more days."

Chapter Thirty-Nine

THE MEN SPLIT UP QUICKLY and went out on their assignments. Jean-Paul and Murphy were already heading off into the woods when Valerie and Rachel came running out of the hut screaming. Valerie was on the verge on panic. "Help, oh my God help."

"What's wrong?" Jean-Paul asked. Surely, Wolf couldn't have been hidden anywhere in the hut, he thought.

"Where's Sahara? We need Sahara," Rachel panted. Sahara was still beside the hut surveying the supplies when she heard the commotion. She ran over in a flash.

"What's wrong?"

"It's Shon," Rachel and Valerie said.

"What is it?" Sahara asked again.

"I don't know," Rachel said.

A pitiful look crossed Valerie's face. "She's sick. *Real* sick. You have to come look at her."

Sahara raced inside the hut. To say Shon was sick was an understatement. She was sweating profusely and lying on her side in the fetal position. Her arms were wrapped around her mid-section and, right at that moment, she was puking her guts out. Sahara knelt beside her and tried to roll her over.

"Oh," she moaned, between retches. "My head is killing me, and my stomach," Sahara tried to massage Shon's elbow and knee joints.

"No, no, stop, please," Shon screamed. Sahara's fingers felt like steak knives.

Sahara took Shon's pulse. It was racing. Next she felt Shon's forehead. *Jesus, she's on fire,* she thought.

"What could it be?" asked Jean-Paul, who'd come in behind Sahara.

She frowned. "Hard to tell right now. Some type of fever, or maybe a reaction to something."

Sahara knelt closer and rubbed Shon's face gently. "Sweetheart, did you eat anything different last night, anything the rest of us didn't eat?"

Shon just groaned and shook her head no.

Muhammad, who'd been checking the area behind the hut and heard Shon's groans, came bursting into the hut. When he saw Shon he roared, "What the hell?" and ran to her side, nearly pushing Sahara down in his haste. "Baby, what's wrong?" he said, then turned and searched the faces of the other castaways. "What's happening?"

"I think she has some type of fever," Sahara said.

Muhammad was confused. "Huh? How?"

Sahara shrugged her shoulders. "I don't know yet. But everyone has to get out of here and give her some breathing room. I need to figure out what's wrong." She shooed them out of the hut and sent Valerie for some water. Muhammad lingered outside. The guys each patted him on the back sympathetically.

"She's going to be fine," Murphy murmured.

Jean-Paul tried to lighten his spirits. "Hey, she has the best doctor on the island, after all."

"Thanks," Muhammad said, managing a weak smile. He began to pace outside the hut like an expectant father. Jean-Paul and Murphy walked off a bit and quietly debated whether they should go search for Wolf.

"We have no choice," Jean-Paul said matter of factly.

He called over to Sammy, who had been looking up and down the beach.

"Sam, stay here with Muhammad. You two have got to guard the women and the rest of our supplies. I don't know where that sorry-ass Fame went. We're going out to bring back Wolf. Dead or alive."

Dead or alive, my ass, Wolf thought as he peered at them through the thick plants. With the dense trees and undergrowth surrounding the campsite, he was able to spy on the castaways with ease. In fact, he'd been watching them from that very spot for most of the morning. Wolf was seething with anger and the desire for payback. After his escape, he'd first planned to kill Jean-Paul immediately. He went so far as to creep just inside the hut, but couldn't make him out among the others in the darkness. Wolf then thought of burning down the hut. The castaways never knew how close they came to a fiery death. Only the thought of the lovely Sahara stopped Wolf. He had other, nastier plans for her. But he would wait silently until dark to get his revenge.

Somebody is going to die today.

Chapter Forty

BY MID-AFTERNOON, there was still no sign of Wolf—nor of Jean-Paul and Captain Murphy. Back at camp, the castaways hoped the two men weren't lost or, worse, dead.

They weren't dead, just dead tired. For hours the two had pushed and trampled their way through the unforgiving forest. They were sweaty and nicked up from dozens of sharp-edged plants and insect bites. Exhausted, they finally turned back. But it would be nearly dark by the time they returned to camp.

Meanwhile, Shon took a turn for the worse. With Muhammad by her side, she cringed in pain for hours. Sahara had made a preliminary diagnosis that Shon had contracted dengue fever, but she couldn't be certain without a blood test. Outside the hut and away from Shon, she explained to the other castaways that dengue fever was a flu-like viral disease spread by infected mosquitoes. To that extent, they were all at risk, but the disease couldn't be spread from human to human. She told them that dengue occurs in most tropical areas of the world, but is particularly widespread in the Caribbean basin, and that it could last from three to ten days.

"How do you treat it?" a nervous Fame asked as he buttoned his shirt up to his neck.

Sahara shrugged. "There is no treatment. Shon just needs rest and plenty of fluids. Which we are running out of, however."

"Could she die?" Valerie asked.

Sahara had the matter-of-fact bearing of a seasoned ER doctor.

"Depends on its progress," she answered. "It may lead to dengue hemorrhagic fever."

Rachel made an ugly face. "Hemma what?"

"Hemorrhagic fever. It's when vessels break and blood starts leaking from the nose or mouth, causing shock and possibly death."

The castaways cringed at the description.

"That shit sounds like Ebola," Fame said.

Sahara shrugged. "It's just as deadly."

"What can we do?" Rachel asked.

"Pray," Sahara sighed.

In the hut, Muhammad knelt beside Shon. "Allah, please spare her life, I beg you," he prayed in a soft voice. "I offer my life instead."

He had been holding her hand for nearly an hour. Her grip was steadily getting weaker. He read her passages from her Bible. Shon smiled at him through dry and cracked lips. The Word always gave her comfort.

"God's will," she whispered. "Don't cry, baby."

Her request was futile.

Shon continued to be wracked by stomach pains, but her vomiting had ceased. It had to. She had nothing left to give. Sahara thought it might do her a bit of good if Muhammad stayed with her. The rest of the castaways left them alone, to give them some privacy.

"It's all my fault," Muhammad said. "I shouldn't have brought you."

Shon coughed and flashed a weak smile. "The trip was my idea, remember?"

He nodded and gently squeezed her hand. "I can't lose you, baby. If I do, I am never going back. I can't."

"Nonsense," she said, her voice low and scratchy. "Think about your wife, your kids."

His wife. His kids. That's all Muhammad had thought about since they'd been stranded. Even if he did survive, how would he even explain his presence there?

Muhammad sucked his teeth and looked away. "I'm sure I no longer have a wife."

"She'll forgive you," Shon said.

Muhammad stood up. "How?" his voice rose. "How can I possibly explain that I somehow got stranded on a desert island in the Bahamas when I was supposed to be on a weekend business trip in Atlanta?"

Shon was silent. What could she say?

"Not to mention, that I was stranded on a deserted island in the Bahamas with my beautiful coworker."

Shon put a finger to her lips. "Shush. They might hear you."

"Shush," Valerie said, pulling Sahara away a few yards away from the hut. "They might hear you."

Sahara cleared her throat. "You're right, girl. As I was saying. There is a real good chance that Shon is not going to make it."

Rachel sat down on a nearby boulder, her face in her hands. "This is horrible! We aren't ever going to get off this island. We're going to die here."

Fame walked over and sat down beside her and put his arm around her.

"It's going to be okay," Fame comforted her.

"Ugh! Get off me," she snapped, pushing him off the boulder.

The group all laughed as he fell sideways in the sand. He was like the little brother you loved to beat up on. Fame got up and slowly dusted himself off. "You know the one thing I'ma hate about dying so young?"

Sahara rolled her eyes. "What?"

"That I'ma die a virgin."

The castaways exploded with laughter. "You are so stupid," Valerie said. "But ugly as yo' ass is, I don't doubt that you're a virgin."

The ladies got kick out that. But Fame was impossible to embarrass. He held his arms out wide and asked, "Wouldn't any of you kind ladies like to deflower me before I die?"

Valerie put her hands on her hips. "Not if you were the last brother in the world, much less the last brother on this island."

"Word," Sahara agreed while high-fiving Valerie.

"Whatever," Fame frowned. "None of y'all ain't took a bath in a week, anyway."

They continued to laugh and tease him.

"I got a question," Sammy said. "What is your story, dude? Where are you from?"

"I'm from my momma."

"We know that, but what is your story?"

The others started to echo Sammy, echoing his choice of words, and Sahara came out with a deep-voiced, "Yeah dude, what *is* your story?"

"That's pretty funny, Sahara," Fame said, acknowledging that she had the best impersonation. "Okay. I grew up in California, Inglewood to be exact. I came from a broken home. Our television was broke. Our refrigerator was broke. And my damn daddy was broke," he laughed.

The castaways joined in with hoots and hollers. Fame puffed his chest out. That joke usually killed them at open mic nights at the Comedy Store on Sunset Boulevard.

"Seriously, I had the normal ghetto upbringing. Daddy made me, Momma raised me."

"Any brothers and sisters?" Sahara asked.

"One brother, one sister."

"What do they do for a living?" Sammy asked.

Fame rubbed the stubble on his chin for a few moments as if in deep thought. "My brother is in pharmaceuticals and my sister is a star in the hospitality industry."

Sammy was taken aback. "Impressive. I bet your mother is proud."

Fame nodded. "Yes, sir. But then, she's not the only mother in the neighborhood with a son who is a drug dealer and a daughter who's a prostitute."

The castaways fell silent and stared at each other. They didn't know whether to laugh or not.

Fame just shrugged. "It is what it is."

"How did you escape it?" Sahara asked.

For once Fame became serious. "Who said I escaped it? I'm broker than James Evans. I've had more to eat this week than I did last week, and last week I was at my momma's house! That party at *Atlantis* was going to be my big break. All kinds of industry bigwigs were going to be there. Jay Leno's producer was going to be there. I can't win. Aw, fuck it," he spat, before plopping down next to Valerie.

They castaways were saddened and touched by his story. Even Valerie. She held his hand and softly rubbed it. "It's gon' be alright."

Fame sighed and looked in her big brown eyes longingly. "You really think so?" His voice was low and soft.

Valerie nodded.

Fame tenderly put his arm around her. She angrily jerked it away. "Not *that* all right, motherfucker."

It was nearly dark when Jean-Paul and Murphy returned, and the other castaways greeted the two men like soldiers back from the war. Valerie and Rachel quickly grabbed the guys some MREs, which they wolfed down along with more than a few large swigs of water.

As they began eating, Sahara asked the million-dollar question. "Any sign of Wolf?"

Jean-Paul shook his head no. Murphy wiped crumbs from his mouth and said, "We walked for hours all over the forest, and nothing."

Jean-Paul added, "Ah, but we did find a decent-sized cave about a hundred yards away from here."

"Probably a bear cave," Fame said fearfully.

Jean-Paul gave him a pitying look.

"Oh, and the captain here almost got his ass chewed by a wild boar."

"Ha," Fame teased, remembering his own wild-boar chase. "So why aren't we having pork chops tonight?"

Murphy grunted. "That boar almost had him some captain chops."

Sammy was antsy. "We didn't see any sign of Wolf along the beach, either. He really covered his tracks well."

"He's out there somewhere and he's coming back. We're going to have to stand guard tonight," Jean-Paul said.

Fame gave a mock salute. "Great."

"And this time," Jean-Paul added, looking directly at Fame, "two men on at the same time. We don't want a repeat of the last time you were on guard."

Murphy motioned to the hut. "What's the latest on Shon?"

Sahara sighed. "Not good."

"She has dingo fever," Fame blurted out.

"It's called dengue fever," Sahara corrected him.

Jean-Paul winced. "Will she make it?"

Sahara shrugged her shoulders.

"How is Muhammad?"

"He's been in there with her for the last few hours, crying," Sahara said. "It's in God's hands now."

Chapter Forty-One

BY TWO IN THE MORNING, Jean-Paul's two-man guard duty was working out fine, though there was still no sign of Wolf. All of the men had decided to sleep outside, for protection as well as convenience. As usual, Fame was the only who complained.

"Some of us should sleep in the hut," he whispered to Murphy. "I mean, what if Wolf kills us all? Who is going to protect the women?"

Murphy smiled, suppressing a laugh. "Hey, we know one thing. You won't be protecting anybody but Fame."

Jean-Paul and Sammy had taken the first watch. Three hours on, three hours off. Murphy and Fame were now on the second shift. For obvious reasons, Muhammad was excused from duty, and he remained inside the hut to be near Shon. The second shift was half over and Fame and Murphy sat by the fire trading war stories and smoking the last of Wolf's weed. Jean-Paul and Sammy snoozed nearby.

"And then her husband and grandmother walked in," Fame deadpanned as he passed the rapidly burning joint. His eyes darted back and forth from the woods to the sleeping Jean-Paul.

"H-h-how did you hide the cowboy hat and Zorro mask?" Murphy sputtered. He had to cover his mouth to keep from laughing too loud.

Fame hushed him with a finger to his lips before reaching for the joint. "I didn't. I yelled trick or treat, then jumped out the window."

Murphy nearly choked on the acrid smoke. "You are insane, my man."

Yeah, he's insane all right, Wolf thought as he watched the two men smoke the last of his stash. He was just out of view, hidden behind a clump of especially thick bushes. *Keep laughing. We'll see who laughs last.*

"Shush," Fame froze. "Did you hear that?"

Murphy sat still with his eyes wide, totally alert. "No. What was it?"

Fame giggled. "Must be da po-leeces."

While Fame and Captain Murphy continued to "out story" each other, they never noticed Wolf tiptoeing through the brush, approaching closer and closer to the hut. He stopped every so often to scan the area for his lost weapons. He emerged just behind the hut, out of eyeshot of the men around the fire, and slowly stood and peeked through the window. Through the moonlight he could tell that everyone was asleep. His eyes gravitated toward Sahara. He observed her outline in the dark and licked his lips.

I am going to make you beg.

Shon shifted onto her side and let out a moan. Wolf quickly ducked down out of sight. He slowly rose and watched her. Shon was lying next to Muhammad. She was in obvious pain.

One less for me to kill. Wolf smiled before tiptoeing back into the woods.

Chapter Forty-Two

SAMMY THREW ANOTHER ARMLOAD OF TWIGS on the campfire. He jumped back from the roaring flames, but the heat was welcome. It beat back the unusually cool breeze blowing through the camp. It was just after dawn and light began peeking through the cloudless sky, illuminating the beach and Jean-Paul, who was stretching and observing the surf. What he saw from the beach worried him. He motioned for Sammy to join him.

"Those are some ominous-looking waves," Sammy said.

"You think a storm is coming?" Jean-Paul asked him.

"What do you think?" Sammy asked. "I don't like those waves, but look at that sky. It's beautiful."

Jean-Paul nodded and mumbled, "Always calmest before the storm, right?"

The guys turned quickly at a rustling sound from near the hut. They gripped their weapons. It was only Sahara.

"Hey guys, what's going on?" She yawned.

Jean-Paul pointed at the whitecaps off in the distance.

"A storm, huh?" she asked.

"It is hurricane season."

They jumped at the sound of Murphy's voice. He'd walked up beside them to get a better look. "The water's rising too," he said, squinting.

"What do you mean rising?" Jean-Paul asked.

Captain Murphy walked down near the surf and bent down. "It's low tide, but look where the water is. It's supposed to be way out there."

"So what are you saying?" Sammy asked.

"That whenever this storm hits, it's going to flood."

Sammy nervously looked at Jean-Paul and Sahara. They knew what he was thinking. They were thinking it, too.

"But the hut is on high ground," Sahara replied.

Murphy frowned. "Don't matter. A good storm surge will flood this whole area. Plus, that hut isn't made of anything more than twigs. No way it will stand up in a fierce storm."

They stood silently and brainstormed for a few seconds before Jean-Paul snapped his fingers excitedly.

"That cave!"

"That's right—the cave we saw yesterday," Murphy replied excitedly. "It's far enough inland and should escape a flood, and it's made of rock."

"Thank the Lord," Sahara said. She was thinking of what Shon would have said, and trying to imagine how they could possibly move her.

"What about Wolf?" Sammy asked.

"Maybe he'll drown in the storm," Jean-Paul cracked. "When do you think it will hit?"

Murphy twisted his face up. "No way to be sure, out here. It could be hours, could be days."

"Jesus," Sahara said, and began walking toward the hut.

"Where are you going?" Jean-Paul asked.

"I gotta pee," she said, never breaking her stride.

"All by yourself?" he asked, jogging up beside her.

Sahara stopped and put her hands on her hips. Her eyes flashed with anger. "I've been going that way since I was a little girl, thank you."

Jean-Paul threw his hands up. "Sorry. I just meant that with Wolf around, it ain't safe for you to be walking in the woods by yourself."

"I'm not worried about Wolf. What I am worried about is having to pee in my pants. What am I gonna do? Pee in front of you?"

Jean-Paul smiled.

"In your dreams," she snapped and walked off.

"I'll be just over here," he called after her.

She halted. "If I so much as hear a leaf rustling, I will be *pissed* off."

As Sahara made her way around the back of the hut to relieve herself, she kept glancing over her shoulder. Jean-Paul was trying to stay out of sight, but she could see him, trailing her like a shadow.

"What are you, my bodyguard?" she called. "It's broad daylight."

Unmoved, he just stared at her with a blank expression on his face. She sighed and parted the thick bushes until she was hidden from view.

"Turn around," Sahara yelled through the bushes.

Reluctantly, Jean-Paul turned around but kept glancing back toward the bushes.

Sahara pulled her jeans down and squatted, but she felt too uncomfortable knowing Jean-Paul was so close by. Frustrated, she pulled up her pants and stomped off further into the forest.

"Bodyguard my ass," she huffed. "Don't need no damn man to watch over me while I pee."

Satisfied that she was alone, she started to unzip her jeans.

Sahara never knew what hit her.

"I got you now, bitch," Wolf whispered. "This is what you call strong-armed robbery."

He cupped one hand over her mouth and the other tightly around her waist, her feet dangling as he lifted her. Her arms were pinned to her sides. She tried to scream and struggle, but it was useless.

"Quit struggling or I snap this pretty little neck."

Wolf's breath was hot and wet. To Sahara, it felt like a like a German shepherd was breathing in her ear. Wolf dragged her deeper into the forest. Sahara kicked and fought the whole way, but she was no match for Wolf, who, though tired and dirty as he was, easily overpowered her. He grinned as he heard Jean-Paul calling for her.

"Damn, how long can this woman pee?" Jean-Paul said, looking at his watch. "Sahara?"

He waited for a full minute before inching closer to where Sahara entered the bushes. A light rain began to fall and thunder could be heard off in the distance.

"Sahara?" he called while looking at the sky.

Emboldened with worry, Jean-Paul parted the bushes. No Sahara.

"Oh shit!" he yelled. "Sahara?"

His heart started racing as he frantically searched the immediate area, yelling Sahara's name. Seconds later, Sammy and Murphy burst through the woods.

"What's wrong?" Captain Murphy asked.

"It's Sahara," Jean-Paul said. "She's gone."

"Damn," Sammy said.

"Whaddaya mean gone?" It was Valerie. Right behind her stood Rachel and Fame. The commotion had awakened them.

"She was right here, you k-k-know?" Jean-Paul stuttered. "Doing her b-b-business."

"She was pissing behind the hut?" Fame asked. "I mean, she was so close to the hut?" The comedian flinched as Jean-Paul made a motion to slap him.

"Shut up," Jean-Paul ordered. "Y'all fan out and follow me. Keep close and if you see anything don't hesitate to yell."

Meanwhile, deeper into the woods, Wolf was savoring the moment. Sahara lay in the dirt helpless, bound and gagged with torn-up clothes Wolf had stolen from their camp. She wanted to gag from the nasty and sweaty piece of cloth that Wolf had stuffed in her mouth. She shuddered to think what it once covered.

"Where's your bodyguard now, bitch?" Wolf asked.

Sahara looked at him with murder in her eyes.

"Tough, eh?" he smiled. "We'll see how tough you are in a minute." He bent and began to pull her jeans down. Sahara gave him no assistance. Wolf slapped her.

"Quit moving, bitch."

Wolf stopped for a moment when he heard what he thought were voices in the distance. He quickly surmised that her rescuers were way off the mark. More thunder crackled in the distance and the raindrops became fatter.

I can't wait until they find her, he smiled. *She'll be all wet.*

Sahara continued to thrash while Wolf struggled with her jeans. He quickly pulled them just below her waist.

"Damn," he said, excitedly grabbing a handful of her shapely ass. "No drawers either."

Thick veins bulged in Sahara's neck as she struggled. Wolf ignored her muffled epithets. He yanked up her T-shirt and fondled her breasts like he was an inmate fresh out of jail. Then Wolf pulled his own pants down. Sahara's eyes widened with fear when she saw that Wolf would not be having a problem with performance anxiety. It took all the strength Wolf had to turn Sahara over on her stomach. He took a moment to stand and admire his prize and free his legs of his pants.

The unmistakable boom of a .357-caliber gunshot blasted through the bushes. The bullet crashed into Wolf's shoulder, spinning him around enough to see the shooter and the wisps of smoke rising from the large barrel. Shock and pain registered in his bloodshot eyes as he feebly tried to charge his assailant.

The next blast opened a hole in his chest that was big enough for a circus lion to jump through. Wolf crumpled and fell to the ground like a wet sack of rice. The rain was falling steadily now, and it turned his freely running blood a murky shade of burgundy. Sahara stared at the shooter the way trapped settlers once looked at the U.S. Cavalry.

If Sahara's mouth weren't gagged, the person holding the gun would have heard her ask, "You? You had the gun all along?"

Chapter Forty-Three

MOMENTS LATER the rest of the castaways came crashing through the trees and bushes. Their jaws dropped at the sight of a dead Wolf slumped at the feet of a half-naked Sahara. But what really caused them to question their own sanity was the missing gun held firmly in Sammy's hand.

"Oh shit," Fame said. "Sammy had the gun?"

Shocked, Valerie put her face in her hands. "I don't believe it."

Thank you God, Rachel thought.

"He had the gun the entire time," Murphy said in amazement to no one in particular.

Sammy heard none of this. He stood frozen with a dead, faraway look in his eyes. Jean-Paul knew the look. Combat veterans called it *the thousand-yard stare.* He'd seen it in plenty of his comrades during Desert Storm. Sammy was in shock. Jean-Paul slowly made his way beside him and gently eased the gun from his hand. Sammy remained motionless. Meanwhile, once they recovered from their own shock Rachel and Valerie ran over and pulled Sahara's pants up while Jean-Paul untied her and helped her to her feet. She fell into his arms, hugging him and crying. Jean-Paul held her tight and wiped away her tears.

"It's okay," Jean Paul comforted her. "He's dead now."

Murphy pushed Wolf's body over. The gaping hole in the corpse's chest was all the confirmation everyone needed that Wolf was truly dead. Sahara looked at the body, spat on it, and then kicked Wolf in the balls. She then walked over to Sammy and hugged him fiercely.

"Thank you," she cried. The other castaways crowded around and slapped Sammy on the back and cheered as though he had scored the winning touchdown in the Super Bowl. All the attention finally snapped him out of his stupor.

"What happened?" he asked, still a bit dazed.

"Dorothy, you killed the wicked witch," Fame joked. "The wicked witch is dead."

Sammy's was confused. "Huh?"

"You shot Wolf," Jean-Paul explained.

The castaways parted, exposing the body.

Sammy scratched his head. "Man, I don't know what came over me. I saw him getting ready to assault Sahara. I didn't even think. I just pulled the trigger."

"I'm glad you didn't think," Sahara smiled, her hair now a wild mess from the driving rain.

Jean-Paul asked what everyone was thinking. "How long have you had the gun?"

Sammy looked at the ground. "Ever since Wolf lost it."

"How did you find it?" Valerie wanted to know.

"When Wolf and Fame went swimming, I saw Wolf hide it in a clump of small bushes by the hut. When he dove into the water, I took it."

"Why didn't you tell anybody?" Sahara asked.

He shook his head. "I don't know. I guess I just thought it would cause more trouble if people started fighting over it. I figured the best thing would be if no one knew where it was."

Murphy looked at the sky, wiping his wet face as it was splattered by the sheets of rain. "We need to go—the storm is getting close."

"You're right," Jean-Paul agreed. "We need to get our stuff from the hut before it hits."

"What you talking about, Willis?" Fame asked. "Where we going?"

Jean-Paul rolled his eyes. "To the cave Murphy and I found."

It was Valerie's turn to ask a question. "Why?"

"Because we will drown if we stay at the hut," Jean-Paul said.

Fame snapped his fingers. "Works for me! Let's get the hell outta here."

As they made their way through the wet and soggy forest, Sammy whispered to Fame, "I've never killed anybody."

Fame slapped him on the back. "Well Samuel, you are no longer an Uncle Tom. You are now Nat Turner, certified field nigger and revolutionary."

They all let out a hearty laugh.

Chapter Forty-Four

BY THE TIME the castaways slogged back to the hut, the wind was starting to whip. The rain made the sand feel more like quick-sand. The rising ocean was getting closer to the hut.

"Make sure to get the MREs and water," Jean-Paul yelled over the deafening sound of the waves. Sammy and Fame grabbed the supplies while the rest of the castaways ran into the hut to get whatever they could salvage. What they saw caused them to freeze. Muhammad was crying and rocking back and forth while cradling Shon in his arms like a baby.

"Wake up, baby, please wake up," Muhammad kept whispering.

From outside came booming thunder. Shon was eerily still. Sahara ran over to check Shon's pulse.

"Get away from her," Muhammad barked. "She's just sleeping." He continued to caress her hair.

Frowning, Sahara ignored him and reached for Shon's wrist. Muhammad pushed her away, almost knocking her down. Jean-Paul stepped in.

"Let her help you," he said firmly.

Sahara stood, dusted herself off, and sighed. "No need. She's dead, Muhammad."

"Dead?" Fame blurted.

Sahara nodded. Muhammad ignored her and kept asking Shon to wake up. Jean-Paul placed his hand on his shoulder. "I'm so sorry, man."

Valerie and Rachel hugged each other and cried.

"What's going on?" Sammy asked, as he appeared at the door to the hut.

Murphy walked over and whispered to him and Fame that Shon was dead.

Just then, a huge chunk of the thatched roof was ripped off by the howling winds. Jean-Paul looked at Murphy. "We have to leave."

"What are we going to do about Shon?" Sahara asked. The other castaways waited to see what he would say. Jean-Paul rubbed his beard, a pained expression on his face.

"I don't know what can we do," he said. "She's dead, and this storm is about to get completely out of control."

Valerie was having none of it. "We can't leave her."

"If we stay here, we'll die," Jean-Paul explained.

Muhammad looked up at them. Deep sorrow was written all over his face. "Don't worry—I'll stay with her."

"Muhammad, come on," Jean-Paul said. "You're crazy. You'll never make it."

"I don't care. I don't have anything to live for now."

Another huge piece of the hut blew off, and more rain came streaming through the opening.

"We *have* to go, *now*," Murphy said.

Jean-Paul told Murphy to take the other castaways to the cave while he tried to talk to Muhammad. He'd catch up to them in a minute. After they left, he knelt down beside Muhammad.

"Guess what?" he asked.

Muhammad ignored him.

"Sammy killed Wolf," Jean-Paul said.

That got Muhammad's attention. "Really, how?"

"He shot him."

"Shot him?"

Jean-Paul nodded, and briefly told Muhammad what had happened.

"The Uncle Tom saved the life of a black woman?" Muhammad muttered.

"Sammy had the gun all along. Can you believe that?"

Muhammad shrugged and went back to stroking Shon's head.

Jean-Paul chewed his lip for a moment. "Muhammad, Shon was such a wonderful person. Her faith was like a light, even when everything looked so dark here. I can't imagine what you are feeling right now. But you have to let go. This storm is serious, and if you stay here it's going to drown you. Come with me and save yourself, man. Think of your family back home. Would Shon want you to die?"

"Jean-Paul," Muhammad said, his face stony. "I really respect you and I appreciate what you just said. But I am not leaving. That's it. If I die, then it is Allah's will."

Jean-Paul sighed. For a moment he thought about knocking Muhammad out and dragging him along with him. But instead, he reached out his hand. "Good luck, brother." Muhammad took it, and they shook. "I'll pray for you." He ran out the door to the sounds of the hut being ripped apart by the winds.

"And I will pray for you," Muhammad softly said, as he crouched over Shon's body, the hut coming apart around him.

Chapter Forty-Five

NIGEL SPENT THE BETTER PART OF THE DAY searching the waters in the direction the Coast Guard had told them about. They came across a few patches of remote beach but saw no sign of the castaways. As the time neared late afternoon, there was a distinct change in the weather. A strong wind blew up and the ocean became very choppy. The guys could see off in the distance that a big storm was brewing.

"What is that? A hurricane?" Mike asked.

"No, probably just a big storm." Nigel cautioned.

Mike squinted hard at the large, ominous clouds. "That looks like it's more than *just* a big storm. What is the radio saying?"

"It's broken."

"Broken?"

"Yeah," Nigel said dismissively. "But I have a portable one."

Henri rolled his eyes. "Well then, man, where is it?"

"Batteries are real low—we can only use it during an emergency."

Mike sighed. "Look at those clouds. This doesn't count as an emergency?"

"Just a big storm," Nigel assured them.

"Shouldn't we head back to the mainland?" Henri asked.

The captain looked at the sky, took off his cap, and scratched his head. "From here, we're closer to the Out Islands. If we head back, with this kind of wind it may take us days to reach the mainland again."

"What about the storm? We can't stay out here," Mike said.

"Don't worry. I know a place where we can ride out the storm," Nigel said, smiling as he wheeled *Queen* in the opposite direction.

If Nigel's radio had been working, the men would have certainly heard the hurricane warnings. They would also have heard that the outer rain bands of Hurricane Henry were ravaging the Turks and Caicos, parts of Puerto Rico, and the British Virgin Islands. So far seven deaths had been reported already. The storm was nearly two hundred miles in diameter, most of it in the Atlantic. The winds were up to 125 miles per hour, ripping trees up by the roots. Some of the Bahamas islands were starting to flood. It was too late for Nigel to return to the main island even if he wanted to. He steered *Queen* to another island hideout, which also had a large sheltering cave. Nigel, Mike, and Henri hurriedly stripped the boat of any food and useful equipment, especially the radio and flares. Nigel knew how bad the storm threatened to be, regardless of what he'd said to Henri and Mike. He knew how to read a sky as ugly as the one about to open over their heads. Despite making a very tight mooring bound to a sturdy-looking tree, he didn't expect *Queen* to survive the storm.

"What will we do if the boat sinks?" Mike asked, as though reading his mind.

"Then *we'll* be stranded," Henri replied.

Chapter Forty-Six

BY THE TIME JEAN-PAUL caught up to the rest of group, they were already in the cave. It had taken them nearly an hour to fight their way to it against the intensifying storm. Soaked to the bone, they held tight to the clothing of the person in front of them to keep from getting lost, as if they were members of an infantry platoon slogging through the Vietnam jungle during monsoon season. Jean-Paul's journey had been even more difficult, as the storm turned the ground into an endless stretch of sludge. He stumbled in to find the rest of the exhausted castaways lying sprawled around the cave's entrance.

"We need a fire," Jean-Paul said, surveying the cave. "Or we gon' freeze to death. Gather up whatever dry wood and branches you can find from further back in the cave."

He wasted no time trying to start a fire the old-fashioned way, by rubbing two dry twigs together.

"Where's Muhammad?" Sammy asked.

Jean-Paul paused, then shrugged. "He's staying."

The castaways took in a collective breath.

"There's no way he can survive," Sahara said quietly.

"He doesn't care," Jean-Paul explained.

For a few moments there was silence as everyone reflected on Muhammad's likely fate.

The silence was broken by Fame. He held a large clump of straw in his hands. "I found something! Looks like an old bird's nest."

"Or a bat's," Murphy teased.

Fame dropped the nest like a hot potato.

The other castaways gradually found more straw and a few bits of wood. After what seemed like an hour of careful coaxing, Jean-Paul managed to get a few sparks to ignite the straw, and not long after that there was a nice fire going. The hurricane, if anything, seemed to be still gaining strength outside. The castaways huddled close together, their shoulders hunched, spent from the traumatic events of the day.

"I can't believe that Shon and Wolf are dead," Rachel said. It was the thought on everyone's mind. "It feels like a dream."

"More like a nightmare," Valerie added.

"Amen," Jean-Paul said.

Fame stretched his legs and yawned. "Maybe they were the lucky ones."

Sahara sucked her teeth in disgust. "Why would you say something dumb like that?"

"Cuz we're all going to die on this goddamn island."

"Shut up, Fame," Jean-Paul said.

"Why?" the comedian asked. "Don't tell me you haven't thought about it. We're on this godforsaken island way out in west bum-fuck. No chance of getting rescued. We have enough food and water to last us a day or two. Then what? We're either killing each other or dying from disease. Who's next to die?"

Jean-Paul stared at him hard. "You are, if you don't shut up."

"Well, I never thought I'd die on a deserted island," Sammy said, trying to break the mood

"Why? How did you think you'd die?" Murphy asked.

"In my sleep," Sammy joked. "Surrounded by my great-grandchildren."

Fame laughed and slapped his knee. "Great-grandchildren? Sheeiiit! A black man is lucky to make it to thirty-five."

"I've always wanted to die at sea," Murphy said.

"I've always wanted to die having sex," Fame cracked. "That way I can *come* and *go* at the same time."

Rachel shook her head pitifully. "You guys are morbid. I'm going to sleep."

"Me, too," Valerie said.

"Hey doc? What happens when you die?" Fame asked.

Sahara scratched the back of her head. "Well clinically, death is defined as the irreversible cessation of all respiratory, circulatory, and brain function."

"Can you repeat that in English?"

Sahara rolled her eyes. "You stop breathing, your heart stops beating, and your brain shuts off."

"I don't think anything happens when you die," Captain Murphy said.

"What—you just die?" Jean-Paul asked.

"Yeah."

"No way," Sammy said. "What about your soul?"

Murphy held out his hands palms-up as if to say, "Who knows?"

"What about heaven and hell?" Fame asked.

"I don't believe in any of that," Murphy said.

Fame hurriedly scooted away from him. "Oh Lord, please don't light his ass up in here."

The captain was unfazed. "That whole heaven and hell thing is a bunch of mumbo-jumbo the Catholic Church came up with to control the masses."

"That's interesting," Sahara said. "But I still believe that if you're not saved when you die, you're gonna burn."

"Me too," Sammy added. "If there isn't an afterlife, what's the purpose of living?"

"God's cruel experiment," Murphy sighed.

Fame stood and looked at everyone around the fire. "Guys, I just wanna say, if I die, I want you know that I am glad I met you all," he said somberly, before adding, "Except for Wolf's black ass."

Sahara pulled his arm. "Sit down, fool. Nobody else is dying."

"Man, life sucks," Fame said. "I mean you're born, you have to go through all the bullshit of living, paying bills, getting old or getting sick. For what? To die? There has to be a payoff."

There was silence around the fire, until Sammy said, in a voice so quiet it was almost as though he was talking to himself, "What do you think is happening to Muhammad?"

Muhammad was oblivious. Outside what remained of the hut was pure swirling chaos. Numb with grief, he couldn't feel the winds of more than a hundred miles an hour wiping away his tears, along with his surroundings. Although he was soaked to the bone, he paid no attention to the sheets of rain pouring into the structure like a waterfall. Muhammad's only thoughts were of Shon. Through it all her cold form remained cradled in his arms.

"I'm so sorry, baby, I'm so sorry," he whispered. "Please forgive me."

Muhammad never noticed the floodwaters rising around him. He didn't feel it when what was left of the hut was lifted off its flimsy foundation. He didn't notice the twenty-five-foot storm surge crashing down on top of him. He never even realized that he had drowned. Through it all his arms stayed wrapped around Shon's body.

Chapter Forty-Seven

THE NEXT MORNING, Sahara was the first to wake up. She squinted to shield her eyes from the sunlight streaming into the cave. For a moment she tried to focus, not knowing if she was dreaming. She rose and tiptoed outside, careful not to wake anyone else. What she saw took her breath away. The dense jungle area all around the cave looked magical. The orange glow of sunlight sliced through the tiny spaces between the trees, leaves, and plants, sending streaks of light in all directions. Sahara closed her eyes and drank in the warmth of the morning.

"Looks like an enchanted forest, huh?" Jean-Paul whispered from just beside her.

Startled for a moment, Sahara flinched. "You scared me," she said, whacking him on the shoulder.

He gave her a sheepish grin.

"You'd never guess a hurricane had just hit this island," she said.

Jean-Paul eased up beside her and slid his hand into hers. After a moment's pause he said, "Sahara. When we get off this island I want to get to know you better."

Sahara was silent, not sure that she had heard correctly. "Huh?" she finally managed to say.

He led her a short distance away from the cave before facing her. "I said that when we get off of this island I want...to...get...to...know... you...*better.*"

Sahara's heart was pounding. "That's what I thought you said," she said, letting go of his hand. "Are you out of your mind?"

It was his turn to say, "Huh?"

Sahara turned away quickly, looking off into the distance. "You're engaged, Jean-Paul."

"A formality," he replied.

"You're crazy," Sahara gasped.

"I think I'm crazy for you," he admitted, inching closer.

Her lips curled into a frown. "You can cut her off that easy?"

Jean-Paul pulled her close and looked into her eyes. "It has nothing to do with her. I knew that my engagement was off the moment I walked onto that boat and saw you."

"The moment you saw my ass," she corrected him.

"That too," he devilishly grinned.

She hit him again, even gentler this time.

"Besides," he went on. "It's basically an arranged marriage. I mean, I, uh, cared about her—but I never really wanted to get *married*. I've done a lot of thinking these last couple of days and I realize now that I only wanted to please my father. Since my mother died, my life is his life. That doesn't mean I should make a big mistake by marrying Nicollete. And that doesn't mean I should give up the chance to get to know you better."

"But I live in Atlanta," Sahara reminded him.

"I'm in New Orleans, that's almost right down the street."

Sahara smiled. "You know Airtran got them good specials to the ATL?"

"No way! I'd walk before I'd fly a discount airline," Jean-Paul laughed.

"Let's start slow," Sahara said sticking her finger into Jean-Paul's chest. "We can plan a trip after you get back and...resolve your situation."

Jean-Paul pulled Sahara close. His mouth pressed up against her ear. He brushed her earlobe. Her neck tingled. "If there is one thing I've learned being stuck on this godforsaken island," he whispered, "it's that life is too short and I have to live my life for myself. Sahara, I know I want to spend time with you. Either on or off of this island."

Sahara held him tight as tears streamed from her eyes. "I feel the same way, too."

Chapter Forty-Eight

T HE CASTAWAYS HAD NO IDEA what they would see when they trekked back to the campsite. However, they were stunned by what they *didn't* see.

"Where's the hut?" Fame asked, astonished.

"What happened to the trees?" Sammy wondered.

"And where's Muhammad? Did he make it?" Sahara added.

Hurricane Henry had devastated their part of the island. Up and down the shore, bent and broken trees were slumped over like old men playing checkers. Some had been entirely uprooted and were floating in the ocean just offshore. Their campsite was erased—the massive storm surge had washed the hut and everything around it out to sea. The bodies of Muhammad and Shon must have been washed away, too. There was no sign of them. Jean-Paul's head hung low.

"I tried to get him to leave," he whispered.

Sahara squeezed his hand. "It's not your fault."

There was silence, which Murphy finally broke. "He may have gotten off lucky," he said, his voice calm but charged with emotion. "At least it must have been relatively quick."

Jean-Paul was too depressed to react to Murphy's dark comments. Rachel, though, did react, by starting to cry hysterically. She wrung her hands as Valerie hugged her tightly, crying softly too. One by one the castaways found places to sit in the sand or on nearby rocks and either cried or mouthed silent prayers. The castaways not only prayed for their dead friends but also for themselves.

"We're all gonna die, I know it," Rachel sobbed.

No one disputed her. Their situation was now extremely bleak. Their water was dangerously low and all that were left were two MREs and a pack of crackers. They were weak and weary. They were unwashed. They were at the end of their rope. Then Fame snapped.

"I can't take it anymore," Fame barked before walking towards the ocean. He was in a trance. He kept muttering, "Fuck it."

Confused, the castaways watched him with wonder. Fame was nearly knee-deep in the surf when Sammy realized what was happening.

"Hey, I think he's trying to kill himself," he said wonderingly.

"Fame?" Jean-Paul called.

"Fame!" the women yelled.

The comedian ignored their calls and continued walking. Jean-Paul, Murphy, and Sammy ran out after him. They nearly tackled him, but the slightly built Fame somehow broke free and tried to swim out to sea. Sammy managed to grab one of his ankles. Murphy pulled at one of his arms. Fame furiously tried to fight them off.

"Get 'em, guys," the women screamed.

It was like trying to catch a slippery fish. After much sloshing around, they finally overpowered him and dragged him to the sand. The women ran over to help.

"Are you out of your fucking mind?" Jean-Paul snapped.

Fame gasped. "I don't care anymore. We're all gonna die anyway."

Jean-Paul shook him violently. "Snap out of it. We're gonna make it."

"You can't go out like that, Fame," Sahara said.

Fame's chest heaved as tears streamed down his face.

It was a desperate scene, despite the beautiful setting. It was another gorgeous morning on their isolated island in the Bahamas. Three exhausted heroes were sprawled out on the sand, muddy and dripping wet. Four women in tattered clothes sobbed in a semi-circle around a suicidal, undernourished comedian. Then, all of a sudden, someone noticed a shark flying in the sky.

Chapter Forty-Nine

Lieutenant Don Shirley had been piloting the *Shark* over various remote islands in the Bahamian chain since dawn without so much as a nibble. It was standard routine for the Coast Guard to inspect these islands after a major storm. So far it was the usual stuff—downed trees, beach erosion. He was ready to steer the *Shark* back to the *Jesse Owens* for lunch when he spotted a group of people clustered on the beach.

That's odd, he thought, and immediately steered toward them. As far as he knew, these islands were uninhabited except for smugglers, and this raggedy-looking group didn't look like any smugglers he'd ever encountered.

When the castaways saw the helicopter they thought it was a mirage. A vision. A cruel trick. They stared at it silently as it came nearer. It was only when the wind from the helicopter blades kicked up a sandstorm around them that they rejoiced. In fact, they hugged and tripped over each other jumping for joy. Then they heard the voice.

"This is Lieutenant Don Shirley, United States Coast Guard. Standby for assistance," the pilot said through the loudspeaker. To the castaways it sounded like the voice of God. Moments later, "Aquaman," the rescue swimmer, splashed down and waded ashore. The castaways rushed up and hugged him like a lost relative.

"Thank you for saving us," Fame gushed, squeezing him tight.

"You don't know how glad we are to see you," Jean-Paul said, shaking his hand.

"How long have you guys been here?" Aquaman said. He had to yell to be heard about the helicopter's racket.

"Don't really know," Jean-Paul said. "A couple weeks."

Aquaman rubbed his chin for a moment. "What happened?"

Murphy stepped up. "The yacht I was piloting had an explosion on board and shipwrecked us."

Aquaman radioed this to Lt. Shirley, and a few seconds later a huge smile crossed his face. "Was your ship *The King's Dream*?"

"Yes," Murphy said, surprised. The castaways were just as shocked.

"We searched for you guys for days after the explosion," Aquaman told him. "But we couldn't find you."

"Well goddamn it, you found us now," Fame laughed.

"Is this everybody?" Aquaman asked.

Some of the castaways looked at each other, others stared at the ground. Jean-Paul spoke up. "No, some of us didn't make it."

Aquaman patted him on the back, paused a moment, then said simply, "I'm sorry."

One by one they were winched up into the waiting helicopter. It took nearly a half an hour for the helicopter's crew to get the castaways on board, and they had to be packed in tightly.

As the helicopter banked away, they took one last look at the island. They thought of all they had lost and left on that remote strip of sand in the middle of nowhere. They lost friends. They left an enemy. They nearly lost hope. But most of all they left a piece of themselves.

"It's tight in here," Fame cracked, trying to eke out a bit of elbow-room. "Like a slave ship."

Aquaman smiled and said, "Like crabs in a barrel."

The castaways looked at each other and then burst out laughing.

"If you only knew," Sahara laughed. "If you only knew."

Chapter Fifty

"I FEEL LIKE I'M DREAMING," Sammy said, admiring the food spread out in the galley of the *Jesse Owens*. There was steak, potatoes, chili mac, fried chicken, and all kinds of cake and pies. Once the crew had learned the castaways were coming aboard, they'd emptied the galley for them. "I didn't think I'd ever eat like this again."

"Me, too," Fame munched. "But y'all ain't got no pig feet?"

The galley crew eyed him hard.

"Sorry," Fame said meekly.

Valerie and Rachel skipped the heavy stuff and went straight to the salad.

"I think I lost ten pounds, girl," Valerie said. "And I want to keep it off."

"I'll help you keep it off," Fame said between mouthfuls of chili-mac.

Valerie gave him the universal "talk to the hand" hand.

Incredibly, Jean-Paul found he was too excited to eat. After a long hot shower and shave, he and Murphy went up to the bridge and debriefed the ship's commander. When Sahara found Jean-Paul, he was looking out at the ocean, thinking of how he was going to break off his engagement with Nikki.

"You know something?" Sahara joked. "You look kinda cute when you clean yourself up."

"And you're the only woman who can make a baggy Coast Guard uniform look sexy."

She did a pirouette. "You like?"

"I like," he smiled.

As they were talking, they could hear a distress call coming over the radio.

"Mayday! Mayday!" the voice squawked through the radio. The voice was distinctively Caribbean. "Me name is Nigel Benjamin, captain of da *Queen* and me lost me boat in da storm." The ship's radioman answered him back and jotted down his position, then radioed Lt. Shirley to head out for the rescue. After the *Shark* launched, the radioman asked, "How many people in your party?"

"Tree, tree people, mon," Nigel said.

"Don't worry, we're sending a helicopter to come and rescue you." The radioman smirked and looked at Jean-Paul and Sahara. "Probably some lost fishermen."

Jean-Paul smiled at the exchange then hugged Sahara. "Fishermen? What could they have been fishing for in that storm?"

The End